Also by Jan Springer

Cowboys Online
Cowboys for Christmas
Cowboys In Her Pocket
Loving Her Cowboys
Cowboys in Her Heart
Always Her Cowboys

Intimate Secrets
Intimate Lover
Intimate Kisses

Kidnap Fantasies
Jade's Fantasy
Zero To Sexy
Christmas Lovers

Pleasure Bound
A Hero's Welcome

A Hero Escapes
A Hero Betrayed
A Hero's Kiss
A Hero Wanted
Captive Heroes

Pleasure Bound Boxed Set
Pleasure Bound : COMPLETE SERIES SciFi Erotic Romance Boxed
Set

Tentacles Shifter Erotic Romance
Taken by Him

The Key Club
A Merry Menage Christmas
Sophie's Menage
Jewel's Menage
Jaxie's Menage
A Homecoming Menage Christmas

The Outlaw Lovers
Jude
The Claiming
Colter's Revenge
Tyler's Woman
Resistance

The Outlaw Lovers
Alpha Outlaws Boxed Set

Vampira
Sweet Heat
Wet Heat
Crimson Heat

Standalone
A Touch of Menage Boxed Set
Shades of Menage Boxed Set
Naughty Girl Desires Boxed Set
Nice Girl Naughty
Sinderella Sexy
The Biker and The Bride
The Fire Within
Bared to Him
Pleasure Bound : A Futuristic Adult Romance Boxed Set
Merry Menage Kisses Boxed Set
Stripped Naked
Risqué Girl Delights Boxed Set
A Holiday Menage
Ménage À Trois
A Hitman for Hannah
Billionaire Boyfriend

Watch for more at www.janspringer.com.

The Fire Within

Jan Springer
Published by Spunky Girl Publishing
Copyright 2014 Jan Springer
Cover Art by Indiebookscovered.com
Edited by Amelia S. Black

The Fire Within
Jan Springer
Chapter One
Year 2100
Sex Squad Headquarters, Vermont, United States

"They call him Loverboy. He is six feet three inches and a hundred and eighty pounds of pure sex magnet. No woman can resist him." Det. Jim McBride's husky voice curled through the briefing room grabbing Detective Sky Kelley's attention.

The two male detectives sitting beside Sky nudged each other playfully and chuckled at Jim's description. Unfortunately, they weren't taking this Loverboy fellow as seriously as they should be. At their interruption, a dark anger crept into Jim's gorgeous brown eyes. "You two giggly boys have something important to share with the rest of us?"

The two detectives frowned and shook their heads in embarrassment.

Jim nodded with satisfaction, and then his intense gaze swooped onto Sky. His eyes softened a bit as he watched her, but the normal laugh lines at the corners of his mouth remained tight.

Bruised shadows hung beneath his eyes. Eyes that used to sparkle with desire for her. Now they held nothing but raw pain.

Hastily, he looked away, leaving her with the impression she was being dismissed as if she were just another one of his "giggly boy" detectives, instead of the woman he had planned to marry...up until a week ago.

Sky closed her eyes for a moment and tried to compose herself. Tears of regret burned at the back of her eyelids. She should have said yes to Jim's demands that they have sex. It would have been so easy to put out that persistent need throbbing between her thighs. However, she wanted to wait until they were married. Unfortunately, she had said no one time too many and now she was alone.

"Here is a little history on Loverboy." Jim said. "Abandoned at birth, he was brought up in an orphanage by nuns. He was groomed to become a preacher, but decided to leave. For the past few years Loverboy has been living on Saturna, the newly formed pleasure planet on one of Saturn's moons."

A wave of excited murmurs echoed throughout the room. Everyone knew about the sex outpost. Several of her friends had said they wouldn't mind taking a trip out there to a world where no one knew them and where they would simply lose themselves in a world of sex. Rumor had it people who went there and walked along the streets could be tapped on the shoulder by complete strangers and they would be obligated to have sex with them. Unbelievable.

Jim continued. "A couple of months ago a young woman went to the authorities on Saturna claiming she was seduced by Loverboy and then kept at a secluded farmhouse against her will while being trained to be a slave. She managed to escape but not before she discovered Loverboy was training other women and men to become sex slaves.

As you, all know, due to the government's need for finding new forms of revenue they have invested heavily in Saturna and it's a cash cow. Sex drugs, prostitution and sex slaves are legal on the planet. However, avoiding payment of the income taxes obtained from such lucrative ventures is illegal. Loverboy has not filed any income tax returns for his ventures on Saturna. If what our source said is true and Loverboy is training slaves, he is in serious trouble for tax evasion, not to mention kidnapping that woman.

The Chief wants two of our detectives to go in undercover as eyewitnesses. One will be a woman. A virgin. A virgin is required because rumor has it Loverboy knows one when he sees one. He can't resist them. And they can't resist him.

Apparently, he is an exquisite lover. Once a woman has been with him, she is hooked on sex. He then gives his victim intensive training. He and one of his orphanage mates, Carmella, are the only instructors in his alleged training school, which happens to be at the secluded farmhouse I mentioned earlier."

The room was deathly quiet. Jim had captured everyone's attention.

"Our source discovered that the slave is guaranteed one hundred percent employment at the end of his or her training period. Payment to the slave is three hundred thousand dollars a year, with an option to continue the contract by either party at the end of that year."

"Get paid and get laid. Sounds like a hell of a good deal to me." One of the "giggly boys" whispered low enough so Jim couldn't hear.

"Beats the pay in the Sex Squad and you can screw your brains out." His companion eagerly whispered back.

Sky shook her head at the detectives' insensitive comments.

How could they joke about such things? Innocents sucked into a life of fast money without waiting to have sex until they fell in love. Was she the only old-fashioned girl left on Earth?

"A thorough inspection of Loverboy's personal villa on the planet showed nothing out of the ordinary going down. We haven't been able to locate the alleged farmhouse being used for the training. Unfortunately our source that was allegedly kidnapped by him disappeared shortly after she reported the incident to the authorities."

Regret whispered through Sky about the missing woman. Loverboy must have heard about her going to the law and taken care of her in some horrid way.

"The victim is an only daughter of a high ranking government official on Saturna. The father has hired us to track her down. The two people who accept the assignment will be given the identity of the woman along with an all expense paid trip to Saturna."

Enthusiastic gasps erupted from the crowd. Jim held up his hand for silence.

"Do you believe she's still alive?" Sky asked.

Jim threw her a cold look and she shivered.

"She's alive. Most likely being trained as we speak."

"So, you believe she's once again being held against her will?" she prodded.

"I mean she may have gone back on her own accord for more sex."

"No man is that powerful over a woman." Sky whispered.

"Loverboy is." Jim stated.

He focused his attention back to to the crowd.

"The other person we need for this assignment is a male detective. He will go in undercover seeking employment as a slave. He must also keep an eye on the female detective while both search for the government official's daughter. Since his villa has already been searched, he will be using the alleged farmhouse or possibly another place."

"What if we can't find the woman?" Sky asked.

Jim looked at her again, his voice stern.

"Then the undercover agents will wait and ask questions without drawing attention to their true identity. They must be prepared to participate in the sex slave training. Without hesitation."

Sky's mouth dropped open in shock. She barely heard the excited whispers from the others shoot through the Briefing room as Jim ripped his gaze away from her and continued speaking.

"The female detective will target Loverboy and the male detective will target Carmella. Your assignment is twofold. Number One, get yourself invited into Loverboy's life and find out if he is in fact training sex slaves. And number two. Find the missing woman and bring her out."

Jim's voice faded into the background as Sky examined Loverboy's surveillance photo accompanying the notes they'd all been given before the briefing had started.

She inhaled softly at Loverboy's sharp blue eyes. They reminded her of a fierce storm. Brooding. Dark. Dangerous. His short feathery blond hair framed a very masculine beach boy face. And those lush lips. So kissable.

A shiver of something quite erotic flickered up her spine. Arousal at simply looking at his picture? Maybe. Or perhaps it was a need.

A need to meet this man and challenge his ability to turn innocent virgins into sex slaves. She wanted to be the one to take Loverboy down...hopefully not on top of her.

*****

"What the hell do you think you're doing taking on the Loverboy assignment?" Jim yelled as he stormed into the secluded conference room Sky was using to study the updated Loverboy brief the Chief had given her after she volunteered for the assignment.

When she lifted her head and stared into his furious gaze, pure liquid-heat streamed through her. He stood so close she smelled his spicy cologne and felt the tension radiating from his body. Dark stubble covered his cheeks and chin adding to his sexiness. Suddenly she wished she'd given into his demands of her making love to him.

An image of her cradled in his strong arms came to mind. Of Jim's powerful hands kneading her tingling breasts. Jim asking her if he could make love to her right then. It had happened on their last date, and they'd been kissing and touching each other in the back seat of his car where they'd gone to gaze at a local lake. His question had frightened her and she'd told him to stop. He had. And then he'd driven her home. At her door, she told her he couldn't wait for her any longer. Their wedding was off and he was moving on without her.

She'd been stunned and devastated.

"You're not taking this assignment. Is that clear?" he snapped. His deep, tense voice brought Sky back to reality and back to the familiar anger, she'd been experiencing since he'd broken things off between them.

"Don't tell me what to do Jim McBride! You lost that right when you cancelled our engagement."

"Oh? And now you'd rather get fucked by Loverboy instead of making love to me?"

"Maybe he'll show me a few tricks," she teased.

His eyes darkened into dangerous slits. She loved it when he was mad. It gave him so much power over her.

A power to do anything he wanted...but he'd never had the balls to do it.

With a quick move that took Sky by surprise, Jim grabbed her around the waist and yanked her clear out of her seat. He captured her startled cry in his mouth as his warm lips crushed over hers.

She could taste his fierce need as his thick tongue slipped into her mouth. Strong and demanding, he probed, pushed, circled and finally mated with her tongue.

Blood roared in her ears. Her nipples tightened and tingled as they flattened against his hard chest.

Many times, she'd been in his arms enjoying his tender kisses. She'd always wished he'd been more aggressive. Today, she just might get her wish. Today, she may have pushed him a little too far. There was a sharp edge to this kiss. A tinge of desperation. A hint of domination.

She liked this new Jim. She liked him a lot and her body melted against him, welcoming him.

Reaching up, she feathered her fingers through his dark brown hair and cupped the back of his head with her hands, drawing him closer. His powerful masculine scent drugged her like a fine wine and his body heat zipped through her thin blouse setting her flesh on fire.

His mouth tasted dark, dangerous and oh so delicious. So yummy she wanted to devour him. All of him.

She ached to taste his chest, suckle his pebble hard nipples and make love to his powerful penis as he thrust in and out of her hungry mouth. The shocking thoughts made Sky shiver with a frenzied excitement. But she should make him stop just like all the other times. This time though, she couldn't. She wanted more from him. So much more.

Her nerves were short-circuiting. Every inch of her tingled. She ached to be touched. To be tasted. To be fucked.

What was happening to her? Oh, who cared? As long as he kept being aggressive.

A noise rumbled deep in her throat. It was a sensual sound she'd never heard before. Jim must have heard it too because his kiss intensified. His lips became more demanding. Dominating. Intoxicating.

She tried to match his strength, but she couldn't. He overpowered her senses and she became lost and mindless with aching sensations she'd never experienced before.

His right hand left her waist and slipped beneath her blouse. In a flash, his fingers dove below the lace material of her bra and headed straight for her left nipple.

He found it. The instant he touched her nipple, blazing pleasure whipped through her breast. Need exploded between her thighs. He squeezed, a punishing pinch. Firm enough to cause a spectacular tenderness to replace the arousal.

Immediately his cruel touch melted into a semi rough caress as he rubbed and rolled her nipple between his thumb and finger. She gasped at the unfamiliar sensations pulsing through her body. His other hand slid tighter around her waist, pulling her closer to him.

She sucked in a breath when his hand left her breast and massaged her other nipple. In moments, both nipples were hard and achy. He moved from her breasts, his hand blazing along her bare belly making her shiver with anticipation. His fingers hooked her waistband. Cool air brushed her legs as he pulled down her pants and underwear.

He cupped her bare ass, lifted her up and plopped her onto the coldness of the table. In one quick sweep, he tugged her pants and underwear off her legs. With one knee, he forced her legs apart and moved between them, pressing his massive yet clothed erection against her exposed and aching pussy.

The size of his bulge frightened her. And it exhilarated her!

She inhaled sharply at the tremors rippling through her. Warm wetness trickled between her thighs, readying her for him. His kiss deepened, tilting her world.

A callused finger skimmed along the inside of her thigh. She shuddered at his touch. It felt so good.

He ripped his mouth away from hers and whispered hoarsely into her ear.

"Don't you realize what you've just volunteered for?"

His finger parted the swollen folds of her labia. He rubbed her clit and an electrifying current shot through her.

She let go of him, threw back her head and cried out from the intensity of his violent touch. She didn't care who heard. She was beyond caring. She'd entered a new world. A dangerous world of desire.

"Loverboy will take one peek at your sweet innocent girl next door looks and fuck you."

Jim's pressure on her nub increased. His touch became electric. Savage.

Sky cried as breathtaking spasms pulsed inside her pussy.

"Is this what you want him to do to you, Sky?"

"Yes!" She hissed.

Her legs trembled as another wave of ecstasy assaulted her. Her hips surged upward against his finger. Begging for more.

She bucked on the table as a finger plunged inside her sopping vagina. White-hot splendor crashed around her. Another burning finger plunged inside. And then another. And another.

He filled her aggressively. His masculine strength hammering in and out.

Faster.

Faster.

Until peak after shocking peak swept over her. They kept coming. Crashing into her. Around her. Waves of exploding heat.

They frightened her.

Jim kept pumping. Her hips kept grinding. She couldn't stop herself!

Something was coming! Something beautiful and scary and fierce. Unbearable pleasure took control.

Sky tightened her eyes. Her heart crashed and she panted.

Jim quickened his thrusts. Within seconds, a deep wrenching explosion ripped through her.

Sky screamed and shivered as convulsions wrapped around her.

"Go with it, Sky. Let yourself go with it." Jim's soft voice urged.

She reached out and clutched his strong shoulders, digging her fingernails deep into his thick muscles.

"Ride with it," Jim whispered.

It was insane. Unbearable. Pleasure. Ecstasy.

Shudders swallowed her. Bright stars burst around her vision and she tumbled into joy. She didn't know how long the frenzy whipped through her, but finally the spasms ebbed. Jim's breaths erupted hard and heavy in her ears. Her vaginal muscles quivered around his fingers.

She was dazed. Wiped out. Satisfied. Wonderfully gratified.

Gosh! That was fantastic!

She held onto Jim's massive shoulders until the erotic flush began to subside. Then she loosened her grip.

"I won't ask if it was good. It's written all over your face. You look like a woman who has been properly finger fucked." His voice was tender and sweet.

Finger fucked. Reality crashed into her. Oh gosh! What had she done?

She sat on a table in a conference room in the middle of Sex Squad Headquarters with a man's fingers impaling her vagina.

What if someone walked in on them? Having sex on the job was illegal. They'd be fired.

Despite her uneasiness, she wanted Jim's warm fingers to stay inside her. It felt so nice. So filling. So natural.

"Sky, look at me."

She opened her eyes and her breath caught at the dark desire.

"Loverboy will fuck you until you're as mindless as you just were. Do you see how easy it is for an experienced man to take down a sexually innocent woman like you? Do you?"

Concern marred Jim's face and doubt filled her. Maybe he was right. Maybe this assignment was too dangerous. Look what had just happened to her. She'd loved what he'd done. She wanted him to do it again.

She almost caved in and told him she would give up the assignment she'd volunteered for. Almost.

"Thanks for the vote of confidence," she said tightly as she realized he'd wanted to teach her a lesson and not please her.

A muscle in his jaw twitched as he studied her. He truly seemed to care for her but she was a big girl. She could handle Loverboy. He must have recognized that she wasn't going to be persuaded into his way of thinking, for he swore beneath his breath.

"Dammit, Sky. Don't do this."

"It's done."

A sucking sound shot through the air as he slid his fingers out of her drenched pussy.

"I guess I was wrong about you, Sky. I'm glad I finally came to my senses and left you. Good luck. You're going to need it."

He turned and stomped toward the door.

Son of a bitch! If he opened that door people might see her like this!

Sky jumped off the table, her shaky legs almost crumbling as her feet landed on the floor.

Quickly she picked up her clothing and covered herself. She wanted to give in to Jim. Wanted him to fuck her and take her back into the world of sexual need. Now!

"Jim! Please, don't go!"

The door opened and he was gone, slamming the door shut behind his broad back.

Too late.

The tiny sliver of hope she'd been harboring about them getting back together walked out the door with him. Wiping away the hot tears streaming down her face, she donned her damp underwear and stepped into her pants.

Gazing at the door, Sky squared her shoulders in defiance.

Jim McBride had just given her a lesson she wouldn't easily forget. She'd be on her guard from here on out.

*****

Jim McBride hunched against the cold brick wall of the deserted men's bathroom where he'd retreated after leaving the conference room and Sky. His heart cracked like a machine gun and his breath escaped in shallow gasps.

Damn! What the hell did he think he was doing trying to change Sky's mind? He should know by now she was one stubborn woman. Once she made up her mind about something, there was no stopping her.

He shouldn't worry about her. Being sexually inexperienced didn't mean she wasn't a good detective. In the line of work she'd always been able to take care of herself. Uneasiness pricked through him. So, why was he apprehensive now? Anything could go wrong, that's why. She was a virgin. Sexually inexperienced. He would lose her if Loverboy got his hands on her.

Jim had read the Loverboy file. The man targeted virgins. He wooed them. Seduced them. Fucked them until they were hooked to his intense lovemaking and then they did whatever he asked. Obviously, he was great in bed if he could turn an innocent woman into a willing slave. There was no way in hell Jim was going to let the woman he loved go down that road.

In desperation, he'd stormed into the room Sky had been using and found her ogling Loverboy's photo, her cheeks rosy red, her big blue eyes wide with want.

She'd looked so desirable. He'd wanted her so bad, his cock ached. He'd craved her to be naked. Right there on the desk. Squirming and moaning as he thrust his cock into her. His long fierce strokes plunging into her pussy, making her scream from the pleasure.

He'd wanted to worship her. To brand her as his own. To remove that expression of interest brewing in her eyes for Loverboy.

The burning anger and her comment about that stranger teaching her how to make love had overruled his usual control to the point where he'd grabbed her and kissed her. Her sweet scent had drowned him and made him heady from sexual need. He'd managed to thwart his own desires in order to please her and she'd melted under his onslaught.

He'd been surprised she'd let him touch her pussy at all. He'd grown bold slipping his fingers past her swollen lips into her hot channel. She'd been tight, but wet with want and had accepted his other fingers with relative ease. He'd begun thrusting into her. Over and over. He'd known the exact instant she'd lost control and given into the desire he was offering. She'd spread her legs wider, grabbed a hold of him, digging her nails into his shoulders.

Jim grinned. He could still feel the sting of where her nails had dug into his skin.

Ravishing agony had scrunched up her pretty face and her guttural moans had urged him on. He'd pumped harder. Faster. Finally, she'd screamed and climaxed, her pussy muscles contracting and spasming around his thrusting fingers.

He'd wanted her to get an idea of what she was missing. Of what she'd been denying him. He'd done the job of pleasuring her quite well. He'd changed her attitude toward sex. Had recognized the magical sparkles of satisfaction in her big blue eyes and the lovely blush of embarrassment on her face when she realized she'd lost control and given him her trust.

Jim closed his eyes at the sweet memory and leaned his head against the cold brick wall behind him. His cock continued to throb with the need for release.

He could still taste her sweet mouth on his lips when he'd kissed her. Could still remember the warmth of her flesh burning into his palm and her warm, wet cream slick on his fingers.

He'd wanted more than anything to remove his fingers and slip his aching shaft into her. He'd been close to doing it. So damn close, but it would have been a mistake.

From the start of their relationship, she'd made it perfectly clear she wouldn't give herself to a man until she was sure she loved him. Then when she'd finally told him she loved him, he'd been ready for sex. But last week she'd said she wanted to wait to have sex until their wedding.

Christ! He'd waited so long to be with her and then she wanted an extension until they got married? She was frustrating.

He craved to make her his wife. Wanted to see her flushed face and to hear those sexy little moans deep in her throat every morning and every night as he made love to her.

He wanted to father her children. If he got his way they'd have lots of kids. There was no way he should let this Loverboy assignment stop him from achieving his dreams. Jim swallowed as an idea hit him. Suddenly, he knew exactly what he needed to do.

Chapter Two
Saturno...one week later

Awareness coursed through Sky the instant Loverboy entered the smoky bar room. He reminded her of a sleek panther hunting for a mate as he strode confidentially to the polished mahogany bar and sat down several barstools away from her. The bartender grinned a friendly welcome to Loverboy and slapped a foamy beer onto the counter in front of him.

Sky didn't miss the appetizing way his skintight jeans hugged his cute buns as he sat on the barstool. She also noticed those extra-large shoes kiss the floor beneath the stool.

You know what they say about a man's feet. Big feet. Big cock.

A spark of excitement shot through her at that thought and her gaze moved up to his frosty beer mug and to his fingers clasped around the glass handle.

Long, thick fingers. Just like Jim's.

Would Loverboy's fingers elicit the same exciting sensations as Jim's? She didn't think so. Jim McBride was the man for her. She knew it deep in her heart, even with the way things stood between them.

Sky swallowed and pressed her cool glass of tequila against her hot forehead. Damn that Jim McBride for pushing her! Ever since he'd finger fucked her, she hadn't been able to think of anything else but sex. Sex. Sex. Sex.

Yeah, sure, she masturbated, but Jim's pleasure had been different. It had been deeper and more soulful and with more meaning. It was as if he'd unleashed her carnal side. Ripped away her confidence and made her addicted to...well, sex.

A friend of hers had once told her, "The minute you get properly fucked by a man, you're hooked. Addicted to the high of sex."

Ain't that the truth.

Over the past week, she'd fantasized way too much about Jim. She dreamed of how it would be for him to make love to her. Having him plunging his hard dick into her vagina or into her eager mouth, or maybe her ass? She closed her eyes and tried to keep the dark fantasies from crowding into her brain. She needed to concentrate on her job and ignore the lust screaming through her system.

Sky rolled her cool glass over her hot cheek, opened her eyes and watched Loverboy.

He appeared different from his photo and from the several other nights she'd followed him since arriving here on Saturno. Tonight, he seemed bigger. More powerful. Damn sexy.

Muscles bulged in his strong arms as he hoisted his mug to his lips. Full lips. Kissable lips.

Down girl.

The next time she saw Jim she'd give him a piece of her mind for introducing her to sex. Up until his impromptu performance, she'd been quite content masturbating on her own and now she had doubts that she could truly handle Loverboy. Earlier, she'd cyber-texted Sex Squad Headquarters to tell the Chief she was making her move on Loverboy tonight and she wanted to know who the male backup would be. He'd reassured her the backup was already in place and she would know him when she saw him.

Her thoughts returned to Jim. Too bad she hadn't seen him since after that episode. She would have loved to flaunt her new style in his face and make him jealous, but she'd been busy getting ready for the assignment. Her last day on Earth had included a complete transformation, which included new clothes and a cut, style and hair color. She'd gone from butt-length mousy brown hair to a stunning mid-back black hair.

For tonight, she'd picked a tight black leather skirt that showed off her wide hips along with a matching pair of pumps, a plain white very see through blouse and a black string bow tie. She'd opted for no bra and no underwear. The latter two were the things she was self-conscious about. The thought of possibly showing Loverboy her pussy in order to get him interested and the fact that her blouse left little to anyone's imagination had her nervous. In the way the male customers eyes had stalked her tonight when she'd entered the bar, she knew she'd done something right.

During her research phase, she'd staked out Loverboy and quickly discovered he was a creature of routine. Every night he visited the same ten bars. He acted like a regular customer and ordered a beer. He chatted pleasantly with a bartender. Ten minutes later, he'd leave. Without drinking his beer.

She'd checked the financial situations of all ten bars and a pattern had emerged. All the bars were owned by the prospective bartenders. All the businesses were in financial trouble.

The way Sky figured it; Loverboy targeted these bars because of their financial distress. The owners kept their eyes open for potential victims and Loverboy paid them generously for their information.

Tonight, she'd picked bar number seven in the string to make her move. It was the smallest business with the largest debt. She'd already given the bartender her sob story over a couple of potent tequilas. Now she waited anxiously for the barkeep to hopefully mention her to Loverboy. It didn't take long.

Unexpectedly Loverboy turned his head and they made eye contact. His look was intense and intoxicating. Her pulse skittered and she forgot to breathe. His gaze slid from her face to skim along the length of her neck, over her chest. She swore she could feel his eyes softly caress her breasts. Her nipples peaked. Hardened. They ached to be touched.

God!

Jim had been right. There was something about this man or maybe the bartender had slipped something into her drink to make her more aware of him. Nonetheless, she needed to be very careful.

Suddenly he lifted his beer mug and toasted her. He followed up the toast with a couple of long sips. Okay, *this* was different. Something was up. She tensed as he placed the mug back onto the bar, nodded to the bartender and then slid off his stool. A moment later and he was heading straight for her!

"You're a beautiful woman obviously in need of a man," he whispered into her ear as he sat down on the barstool beside her.

His breath smelled delicately of beer and it mixed with his own unique scent that went straight to her head like a shot of whiskey. A tinge of dizziness swept through her and she held tight to the edge of the bar.

Easy girl. You're here for a reason.

Sky swallowed. Hard. She looked up at him under her lashes and smiled seductively.

"What makes you think I'm in need of a man?"

"The way your nipples are practically popping out of your blouse. Aching to be caressed. Suckled. Worshipped.

Mercy! He had a way with words.

He continued, his breath a whisper, "Your eyes are shining brightly with a hunger for sex. I'm sure if I touched your vagina, you'd be wet for me."

"And if I reached over..." Sky swallowed back her fear and forced herself to keep her eyes on his sexy mouth as she boldly cupped his giant bulge pressing against his pants.

The man was huge! Almost as big as Jim. She squeezed his hard erection and Loverboy's lips twitched slightly.

Amazing. A tough man like himself, aroused by her touch.

Feminine power surged through Sky and it gave her back some of that confidence she'd lost to Jim when he'd finger fucked her last week.

Sky's smile grew.

"Your place or mine?" she asked as she released her grip from the intoxicating bulge.

Loverboy returned her smile.

Gosh, he looked cuddly when he smiled like that, but she noticed his smile didn't reach his cool blue eyes.

"I'm sorry, I don't do virgins," he suddenly said.

Sky blinked in surprise. Was he testing her? Suddenly she could feel the Loverboy case begin to slip through her fingers.

"Excuse me?"

"I'm sorry," he said. "I've offended you."

"No. No. I'm the one who's sorry. I came on too strong. I've never done this sort of thing before. Temporary insanity. A momentary lapse of judgment."

Heck, she'd never expected he would turn her down. She fingered the condensation on her tequila glass and wondered what she should do next.

"That's quite understandable," he replied. "You want to get back at your ex-fiancé. Show him you've decided you'd rather get fucked by someone else because he couldn't wait for you."

He was using the information she'd given to the bartender. She smiled as sweetly as she could under the circumstances.

"That's very perceptive,"

"Actually, the bartender mentioned you had some trouble with your boyfriend. It's very admirable you wanted to remain a virgin until your wedding. He should have been very proud to wait for you and to be given the privilege to experience where no other man has gone before."

Despite trying to appear sophisticated, she couldn't stop the hot flush flooding her face. When she'd sobbed her story to the bartender about getting dumped because she wanted to wait until she was married, she hadn't been the least bit embarrassed. What she'd told him was part of her strategy in getting noticed by Loverboy. She'd stuck to the truth as much as possible, lessening her chances of saying the wrong thing and tipping off Loverboy she was a Sex Squad cop.

"Ah. A virgin blush. The most beautiful thing for a man to see."

"I intend on rectifying that problem soon." Sky stated.

"So the bartender told me."

"And since you don't "do" virgins..." Sky studied the smoky room. "I'm sure there will be another candidate along soon enough."

"I think maybe I can help you...in some other way."

She narrowed her eyes and tried to appear curious.

"How?"

"The bartender mentioned you got laid off last week. I may be able to find you employment."

She faked excitement. "Are you serious? I am so desperate for work. I'm weeks behind on my rent and my land lady says I have until tomorrow night to pay up in full or I am out on the streets. And you know as well as I do that Saturna is not a place to be homeless."

"I run a school in the area."

Bingo. Sky ran a finger leisurely along the edge of her glass and tried hard not to show her excitement.

"What kind of school?"

"How to "please" men and women."

"Excuse me?"

"I plan on training sex slaves for Saturna. I'm searching for recruits. Are you interested?"

Her heart picked up speed. "I've heard they make great pay."

"They do."

"I might be interested."

"What's your name, hon?"

"Sky. Sky Blue." It was the cover name the department had come up with for her.

"How about you come to my farm and meet the class? You can participate in some lessons and if you don't like it, you're free to leave".

"How do I know you're not just going to take me out somewhere, fuck me, kill me and get rid of my body?"

Loverboy grinned and shook his head slowly.

"That would be bad for my business. Everyone here sees me talking to you and if you leave with me, they'll see that too. If you go missing, there are plenty of witnesses that saw us together. The last thing I need is to have the cops asking a lot of questions and scaring off potential clients, right?"

Sky nodded. "I suppose."

"So, do want to try out the school?"

"On one condition."

"Anything."

"You buy me one more Tequila for the road."

Heaven knew she was going to need it.

*****

Although Sky felt flushed, she didn't think it had as much to do with the drinks she'd had as it did with this virile man sitting on the truck bench seat beside her. There was something about his scent that made her heart gallop at full speed with both excitement and fear.

Her ploy had worked. She'd been invited to Loverboy's farmhouse. But what if he decided he did "do" virgins and wanted her?

Although she knew self-defense, she didn't know if she could fight this big guy off her if he decided he did want her.

"Where are you from, Sky?"

"New Hampshire, Earth," she lied.

He frowned. "That's not far from where I grew up. Just across the state line, actually." He became quiet for several moments before speaking again. "How long have you been here? What kind of work were you doing here? I gather from our conversation you don't work in the pleasure business as that's what this planet is all about."

Perfectly normal questions. So why were beads of perspiration popping out on her brow?

"I worked for my fiancé. He ran several pleasure houses, but he sold them and returned to Earth just last week. I worked as a receptionist at one of his houses, hence why I am out of work now." She'd supplied the information as part of her cover. If he checked it out, everything would seem legit.

"Any family?" he asked.

"Mom was it." She'd agreed to stick to the truth regarding family life. Less to memorize. "Mom died a few years ago. Way too old for her age. Worked herself to death juggling three jobs so she could bring me up with the things she never had."

"And your father?"

Sky forced herself to keep her anger in check at that question.

"Never knew him. He took off when he got mom pregnant. He joined the army and she never heard from him again."

"I see."

Sky inhaled a quiet sob as she remembered her childhood. Her mom had dragged her all over the States, working here and there. Doing a little prostituting when funds were low. She'd even read tarot cards to raise money for food.

"I suppose that's why you've hung onto your virginity so long. Can't trust a man."

"Can't trust condoms or The Pill or The One Year Injection. They aren't one hundred percent reliable."

"Well, there always is that chance that one of those little buggers won't wiggle through and you'll end up like your mom, right?"

Sky nodded. He hit the nail on the head with that one. It was why she wanted to wait until she was married. She'd confessed to Jim all about it, but he'd just gotten pissed off claiming he wasn't like her father.

"Yet you want to lose your virginity to a stranger?"

Although she felt quite jittery and a bit embarrassed at his prying questions, Sky tilted her chin upward in a brave show of defiance. Oh, the things a Sex Squad Cop had to do to take down her man.

"That's right. I aim to get fucked. Good and hard."

Oh God! She couldn't believe she'd just said that.

"You're not afraid to get pregnant anymore?" he prodded.

Sky shrugged. "If it happens, it happens. It's time to get on with my life. I want to experience being a woman."

"Why not ask your ex-fiancé to do the honors? I mean he's been waiting for so long. I'm sure he'd be more than willing."

"He's long gone. Out of the picture. Besides, I don't want to return to Earth. Saturno is my home now. Besides, I don't have the money for the flight back." She wished her backup man was tailing them and keeping an eye on her. She couldn't help but to glance at the side view mirror. No lights beckoned to her.

"I'm sure we can find the right man to do the job, for you. We want your first time to be...memorable."

He glanced over at her and winked.

Sky's breath caught. What did he mean by that remark? Had he changed his mind? Was he insinuating he was going to do the job? What if he offered? What if she accepted? Sky shook her head.

No! She couldn't accept an offer from Loverboy, that is if he made one. She needed to stick to her principles. Besides, she still wanted Jim. But she couldn't help remembering what her cover might require. That, if necessary, she actually become a sex slave in order to infiltrate Loverboy's organization and to find the missing woman.

Sky drew her gaze to Loverboy's long fingers curled around the steering wheel. Wetness pooled in her underwear as she remembered Jim's fingers thrusting into her pussy.

To her surprise, Loverboy lifted his arm and curled it around her shoulders drawing her against him. The urge to pull away was great, but she didn't. The gesture to escape his embrace would only tip him off. Best to stay right here and pretend she was truly interested in him.

Up ahead, in the darkness, a farmhouse appeared. The porch light shone across the yard giving Sky a good glimpse of the building. White paint curled off the walls in long strips, revealing an ugly dark gray beneath. Some shutters were missing, others were crooked. What once must have been a garden lining the front porch was now overgrown with weeds. Although the house appeared neglected, Sky saw the potential.

A few slaps of white paint, some rosy pink on the shutters, pretty wildflowers in the garden and the place would be friendly. A buttery glow splashed from most of the windows and as Loverboy drove the pickup truck into the yard, Sky spied a shadowy figure watching from a second floor window. It quickly vanished.

Two brunettes lounged on a couple of porch wicker chairs and when they spotted the truck, they raced down the stairs toward them. The women were young and very pretty and a niggle of low self-esteem slipped over Sky. They were gorgeous compared to her. They were thin with seductive curves and well toned. Model material. Slave material.

They wore very short shorts and halter tops that left nothing to her imagination. With those gorgeous creatures around him, no wonder Loverboy had refused to fuck her. The smile of appreciation on his face proved Sky's point. She was surprised when annoyance skittered through her the instant the two women latched onto him as he stepped out of the truck. They wasted no time running their palms over his biceps and shoulders and by the smile on his face, Loverboy was enjoying their attention.

How cozy. They are just like clinging vines.

Her cop brain shifted into gear. Who were these two young women? They were barely out of their teens and willing to become sex slaves. Why were they so happy to see him? And why couldn't they seem to keep their hands off him?

"We're glad you're back." The pretty brunette with a heart shaped face said.

"Hi Carmella. Hi Loren. You gals been practicing your lessons while I was away?"

"We have." The brunette said. "Loren was showing the new guy some of what she's learned so far with her tongue." Sky didn't miss the enthusiasm in both their eyes or the reddish glow to their cheeks as they spoke of the newcomer. He had to be her backup from Sex Squad Headquarters and this Carmella chick looked exactly like her photo in the Loverboy file. She had sparkling green eyes and a mole above her upper right lip.

"Did you bring the presents?" Carmella asked.

"In the back of the truck."

The two women squealed and giggled as Loverboy led them to the back and lifted a large paper bag over the tailgate.

From the bag, he withdrew two long white boxes.

Long stemmed roses? Maybe. But she wouldn't bet on it.

Sky climbed out of the truck and joined the happy trio and Carmella acknowledged Sky by giving her a quick visual once over. Without saying hello, she returned her attention to Loverboy.

"I see you've found another student," she said as she tucked her white box behind her back.

Loverboy nodded. "Ladies, this is Sky. She's going to try out some lessons and see if she's interested."

"She's not sure she wants to be a sex slave?" Carmella asked.

"She's pretty sure. It's just she's a virgin." Loverboy said quickly.

Sky didn't miss the pissed off expression Carmella threw at him.

"I see," she said coldly.

"Lessons start in an hour. Spread the word." Loverboy stated firmly.

Carmella stared at him for a long moment and Sky could see irritation flaring in her eyes, but she said nothing. Obviously, there was some discord between the two partners.

The two women brushed past Sky and she noticed the diagrams on one of the white boxes they each held. Loverboy had just given them vibrators.

When the two women slipped inside the farmhouse, he shifted the paper bag in his arms and grinned at her.

"I've already got a mistress lined up for Loren. She saw Loren's photo and fell in love with her. How about you? Do you prefer women over men?"

Shit! What was the right answer?

"Depends who pays more," she answered carefully.

"That's what I like to hear. A woman who is open minded. You'll go far in this business if you don't limit your possibilities."

Sky forced herself to return his smile. He waved his hand in a sweeping gesture toward the building.

"After you," he said.

Sky swallowed nervously as she passed him and the full paper bag he clutched in his hands.

Vibrators! Were they the same kind she used? A delicious seven-inch long dong, one inch wide with the utmost in satisfying power.

Unbidden came a fantasy of Jim lying naked on a bed. Tangled sheets wrapped around his muscular thighs as he kneeled on a bed between her widespread thighs. A tempting glimpse of dark curly hair and a sizeable penis hung from him. Hooded dark eyes seared into hers as he thrust the vibrator into her pussy.

"Seems like the crew has already turned in to prepare," Loverboy commented.

"Prepare?" Sky asked as they entered the farmhouse.

"For their lessons."

Right. Should she ask him questions about the lessons? Or would she appear too curious?

"Don't worry, Sky. I'll introduce you to the lessons slowly. See if you like it. Then I'll give you more details about the job."

Oh dear. How in the world was she going to be able to go through with this? Or maybe the question would be, how far was she willing to go to get this guy?

"Ah, there is the new recruit." Loverboy cooed as he peered up the steep staircase.

Sky followed his gaze and her mouth went dry with shock as she caught sight of a man standing in the shadows at the top of the stairs. Although she couldn't see his face, she recognized his well-built physique. Slim hips, the lean torso, wide shoulders, and those lethal long fingers.

Oh-my-God!

Jim!

Chapter Three

"Would you like something to eat? Or drink?" Loverboy broke into her thoughts.

Her heart pounded insanely in her ears and she realized she'd been holding her breath.

"No thanks...I'm tired. If you wouldn't mind, I'd like to lie down for awhile. I must have drunk too many tequilas."

The sooner she ditched Loverboy, the sooner Jim and she could look around and hopefully find something about the missing woman.

"Jim!" Loverboy called up the stairs. "Would you mind showing Sky to her room? It's the last one on the end of the hall. Right side."

"Sure. Come on up, Sky."

Sky shivered at the sound of Jim's husky voice curling out of the shadows. She was about to start up the stairs when Loverboy asked her to stay a moment.

"Here, this one is for you," he said as he reached into the bag and produced a white box for her.

Her very own vibrator. How quaint. *Asshole*.

"Thank you. I'm sure this will come in very handy," she said quickly, hiding her annoyance.

"Your welcome, Sky."

She watched him stroll through a nearby doorway and disappear. A moment later she heard the excited squeal of females.

What was he? A sex magnate?

Screw Loverboy. She had her own hottie to deal with. Jim was her backup. Why the Chief had eluded to tell her, was a mystery but she was glad he was here. A sweet hum whipped through her at Jim's hot stare as she ascended the stairs toward him. When she neared the top, she noticed he had a new look too. His medium length brown hair had been cut shorter and was now brushed and greased back off his face giving him a bad boy mafia appearance. He wore a black short-sleeved t-shirt, which showed off his powerful muscles. And his jeans being so tight, she easily saw the large bulge between his thighs.

He stood right there in front of her, barring her way with his muscular body. The intense way he gazed at her made her remember her new look as well and the revealing clothes she wore. She'd never seen him gazing at her like this before. It was a possessive stare. A wildly erotic glare. She liked how it made her feel. Feverish and needy and excessively feminine.

His intoxicating male scent swarmed over her, making a deep intimate part of her spark to life. Desire to curl her arms around his neck whipped through her. She craved to kiss away the leashed anger emanating from his magnificent body. She wanted to tell him she was sorry that they fought. But she kept her mouth shut. They had better things to do at the moment.

"You like what you see?" His voice was dangerously calm and low and it made her gaze snap back to those gorgeous brown eyes that oozed naked desire.

"Why didn't you tell me you were the backup?" she whispered.

"Didn't have the time."

His gaze hungrily traveled to her sheer blouse. Then he spoke louder. "You're room is this way, ma'am."

She followed him down the long hallway and watched his nice looking butt cheeks shift against those tight jeans as he walked. Her vagina quivered when she envisioned herself cupping his bare ass as he pressed his hot penis into her.

She inhaled softly, trying to still the rapid beat of her heart. She'd better control herself and keep her mind on her job.

At the end of the hall, Jim stopped, opened a door and flicked on a light.

Sky inhaled at the beauty of the cozy room. Virgin white cutwork linens adorned large windows. Huge pillows edged in scalloped lace lay on the white bed comforter. The bed itself was made of knotty pine with an unusual headboard shaped like a wagon wheel.

Sky walked over to it and ran her fingers over the intricate design on the sturdy spindles.

"It's beautiful. So rustic and romantic."

"A room fit for a princess. And every beautiful princess should have one of those boxes." Jim indicated the white box she held in her hand. Sky's heart picked up speed as warmth once again flushed her face.

He grinned and his sexy smile made her heart do a little double flip. Then, he pressed his fingers to his lips in warning and she fell silent. Something was up.

Listening devices, he mouthed the words.

She nodded her understanding.

"Thanks for showing me to my room. Um, perhaps we can see each other during the lessons tonight?" she teased.

"Looking forward to it ma'am."

He strolled across the floor, opened the door, peeked out to see if anyone was there and then closed the door with enough noise to indicate he'd left her alone. He came back, took the box from her hand, tossed it onto the bed, and then he grabbed her by her elbow and led her into the bathroom.

Closing the door quietly, he turned on the water taps. She dumped her purse on the bathroom counter and followed Jim's gaze as he scanned the bathroom for listening devices or other monitoring systems. When they found nothing, he switched on the bathroom fan as a precaution. Then he turned to her. His clean scent wrapped around her making her want to touch him, but she forced herself to keep her arms to her sides.

"I searched a couple of the bedrooms and found listening devices," he said.

"Obviously Loverboy and Carmella don't trust too easily," she noted. "In their line of alleged illegal activities, I wouldn't either, which makes me wonder why he brought me here without checking me out. And exactly how long have you been here?" she asked.

"Long enough to have not seen Sally Green."

Sky shook her head. "I still can't believe she's the missing woman."

"Daughter of our own Chief, who the hell knew. No wonder he wanted to keep her identity under wraps."

"She is a beautiful young woman. I'm not surprised Loverboy targeted her." Sky said as she remembered the photograph the Chief had given her of his daughter. Loverboy would have pounced on a gorgeous woman like Sally. Voluptuous curves and a seductive smile that screamed fuck me now.

"You did a good job getting Loverboy's attention, Sky, but can you handle what's coming next?"

"What's the matter? You can't deal with a little bit of sex?" she teased.

He bristled visibly at her remark.

"That's an odd comment coming from you, Sky."

Ouch.

"Seems like you're already into this sex game," he continued. "The way you were practically sitting in Loverboy's lap when you two drove up in the truck, I could see the sparks shooting out the windows. If there was a gas leak around here, we would have all been blown to kingdom come."

"We were just getting acquainted. Like you were doing with that Loren woman's tongue."

He arched a dark eyebrow at her.

"You heard about that, did you? Any objections?"

"Why should I care? You're a free agent again. Just like I am."

Sizzling tension whipped through the air between them putting her senses on full alert.

"Do you still want to go through with this assignment? Even if it means you might lose your virginity before you leave this farmhouse."

"Is that a promise?" she asked.

His eyes darkened and its intensity startled her.

"Is that an invitation?" he asked.

"What do you think?"

"Don't toy with me, Sky. You may not like the results."

"You don't scare me, big guy."

A shiver of excitement rippled through her when she read the intent in his eyes. The son of a bitch was going to kiss her. Before she could protest, not that she wanted to, his hands roughly cupped her face and he lowered his head toward hers. His warm mouth sealed over hers in a hard possessive way. A little too hard. A little too firm. A little too perfect.

No more mister nice guy. He was a man who knew what he wanted and the confident way he was kissing her, he wanted her.

She moaned softly, giving into the headiness of his mouth sliding over hers. Her arms slipped around his neck and her fingers feathered into his soft hair.

His kiss intensified, making her feel punch drunk. Need for him made her breath catch. Made her pulse quicken. She parted her lips allowing him access to her mouth. When he came in, the provocative heat of his tongue slammed against hers. She moaned shamelessly at the deep pleasure of their tongues touching.

His trembling hands unbuttoned her blouse while he kept his hot mouth expertly moving over hers, distracting her from wanting to stop him. She savored the sexy flavor of his full lips and she loved the coiled need unwrapping deep inside her pussy.

He tugged her blouse over her shoulders, allowing it to slip off. Cool air breathed over her bare breasts, making her nipples stab into the air. She arched as his hot hands cupped her breasts, his thumbs gently caressing her stiff nipples until they were aching with need. The intimate gesture set her pussy on fire and she wanted him to touch her down there. Like the first time he'd done it with his fingers.

In desperation, she slid her hands from his neck and splayed her palms against his warm chest. His muscles quivered beneath her fingertips as she traced a line downward, brushing her fingertips over the hard muscles of his flat stomach. After following the silky path of curly hair that led to the belt line of his tight pants, she struggled to unfasten the button and sighed into his hot mouth at the crisp sound as she lowered his zipper.

In a few seconds, she would guide him inside her pussy. Oddly enough, where the idea had once frightened her, it now excited her.

"I think Loverboy put something in your drink," Jim whispered as he broke the kiss for a moment and then fused his mouth over hers again.

Something in her drink?

Shouldn't she be...alarmed at that suggestion? She wasn't though. She enjoyed the sharp friction of his chin stubble rasping against her trembling lips. Loved the heat zipping through her body as she pressed herself against him.

On a groan, he broke the kiss and pushed her against the countertop. Dropping his hands from her breasts, he gazed upon them.

"You look damn good, Sky. Damn good." His voice was thick with arousal. A faint smile lifted his lips. "Now I wonder if you taste as good as you look."

She blinked in surprise as his head lowered. His hot tongue shot out and licked her right nipple. The warmth of his rough tongue against her tight flesh startled her. Without warning, he popped her nipple into his moist mouth. Rays of pleasure zipped through her breast making her shiver.

His hand clamped over her other breast. He kneaded her roughly, and suckled her nipple. His mouth was warm and wet. His tongue constantly jabbed at her tender tip, sending sexually charged messages to parts south.

His zipper forgotten, Sky reached up and smoothed her hands over his shoulders, enjoying the cords of muscles there, before cupping the back of his head and pulling his face into her swollen breast. This time she couldn't stifle her cry as his teeth sharply nipped her nipple.

Something untamed and delicious whipped through her, leaving her self-control in ruins and anxious for him to take this even farther.

"Fuck me, Jim. Please fuck me," she gasped.

Her words made his mouth still on her nipple. Then he pulled away.

He stared at her with eyes dark with desire. His pupils flared with need and his breath was raspy and hard.

His Adams apple bobbed as he swallowed. "I want to fuck you so bad right now it hurts. But how do I know you're ready for me? How do I know you won't say no? How do I know he didn't put something in your drink?"

"How do you know I had something to drink?" she asked, quite ready to deny she'd been drugged.

"I can taste it and I can smell it on your breath."

Shoot.

Desperation made her shameless.

"I want you, Jim. More now than ever."

His eyes widened at her answer and she fought to inhale air as the familiar shade of hurt shone in his eyes.

He didn't believe her. He thought she was teasing him?

Sky reached out to him but he backed away. His hands were held up in defensive gesture as if to ward her off.

"You've been drugged, Sky."

She shook her head. "No, I want you."

"Stay in your room until it wears off. Fake being sick if you have to."

Like hell.

"Jim¬..."

"I've got to go. They're expecting me."

Turning away, he quickly slipped out of the bathroom, closing the door behind him.

Dammit!

Sky stomped her foot as frustration whirled through her. Was Jim right? Had the bartender slipped something into her drink making her feel hot and bothered? Gazing into the bathroom mirror, she frowned. Her bare breasts were swollen, her nipples red and taut. Her lips were red and full from his kisses.

She looked pathetic. She looked like a woman who wanted to be fucked, yet devastated because of rejection by her one true love. She'd offered herself to Jim and he'd walked away.

Son of a bitch.

Sky shook her head. She had no one to blame but herself. The next time she saw him, she'd make sure he understood she wanted him. Drugs or no drugs, the next time she wouldn't take no for an answer.

She *should* take a long cold shower. That would fix the problem of her wanting sex with Jim. Or maybe it wouldn't.

Visions continued to swirl inside her mind. Of Jim stepping into the shower to join her. Water sluicing off his naked body. Muscles rippling in his arms as he reached out and cupped her swollen breasts in his big hands. Her, reaching down and grabbing his hot rigid shaft...

Her vagina clenched in response and Sky moaned. The sultry sound ripped her back to reality.

Okay, she'd better skip the shower.

Turning off the taps and the bathroom fan, she then grabbed her blouse. Frustrated, she left the bathroom. Through the dimness that enveloped her room, she noticed the slim white package containing the vibrator where Jim had tossed it earlier.

She licked her lower lip. She was too wound up to be any good right now. Her skin felt too hot and too electrified. Jim was right. Something had been put into one of her drinks.

She needed to take care of business, so she could clear her head. Within moments, she'd locked the door to her room. After unwrapping the toy, she then cleaned it in the bathroom, grateful an energy packet had been included. After she slid off her shoes and her tight skirt, she slipped between the sheets and flicked on the machine.

The low hum from the vibe was music to her ears. She smiled and closed her eyes. All she needed to do was...

She gasped as the vibrator pushed past her puffy pussy lips and rubbed her ultra-sensitive clit. Damn that feels so good. She moaned quietly as she rubbed the round head of the quivering machine in circular motions around her clit. Shivers of pleasure trembled within her. Without hesitating, she slid the huge vibrator away and with two fingers from her other hand, rubbed them against her clit where the machine had just been. As she massaged, she inserted the vibrator into her wet vagina and gasped as her pussy muscles clenched around the intrusion.

Keeping up the strokes to her clit with her fingers, she slowly, erotically slid the vibrator out. Breathing hard, she thrust the vibrator in again and began using long and powerful strokes as she imagined Jim fucking her. Just the thought of Jim making love to her, had her coming. Erotic spasms crashed into her. She shuddered at the intensity, and cried out shamelessly as she rode the pleasure waves, while bucking into the carnal convulsions.

When her orgasm subsided, she forced herself to focus on the quietness sinking into the farmhouse. Beside her bed, a cool breeze sifted through the slightly open window. The whispering wind caressed her hot cheeks and soothed her feverish body.

An bird screeched somewhere in the distance. Leaves rustled and floating through the layers of natural noises, came an odd sound that didn't quite fit.

A creak. Like someone opening a door. Her breath caught in her lungs.

Was it *her* door opening? Had Jim decided to join her? Adrenalin stabbed through her and she sat up in the bed. Along with the surge of excitement came a kaleidoscope of physical sensations. Her heart began to hammer. Her breasts felt larger, swollen, aching with anticipation. Her nipples tingled and throbbed at the same time. A powerful need to be touched crawled along her skin like wildfire. Her body hummed.

Oh great, there was no doubt now, Jim had been right. She wouldn't be here in a strange bed, masturbating, if she hadn't been drugged. This was so not right. Not like her. Yet, she couldn't stop the anticipation of craving sex from slowing.

Shoot! She should have anticipated something like this happening. Saturna, with it's Earthy atmosphere, was a pleasure planet and sex drugs were plentiful and normal here.

She tensed as another creak ripped through the silence. And then another. It was followed by a low, drawn out moan.

Oh great! Someone was having sex. Like was everybody on this planet drugged?

Groaning her frustration, she climbed out of bed. In the darkness, she groped for her clothing. Instead of finding them, her hands touched the wood of the night table where she'd put them. She jolted. Where were her clothes?

Cursing beneath her breath, she searched the area beside the night table and found nothing. She spied a lamp on the night table, and flicked the switch. Nothing happened.

A man's erotic groan drifted through the air making Sky's heart pound harder. Was it Jim?

She listened intently. More groans. She couldn't be sure if it was him. She tiptoed to the door and to her surprise found a flimsy light colored, very short nightie hanging on a door hook.

Her cheeks heated with embarrassment. While she'd been masturbating, someone had entered her locked room and taken her clothing, replacing them.

Opening her door, she poked out her head and listened.

The hallway was alive with moans, groans and squeaking bed springs. She envisioned Jim. He stood in front of her, his body tense with arousal. Muscles laced his nude body. Sky's pulse skittered. Her legs trembled as he studied her nakedness. He held his thick erection in one hand, and with his other hand, he stroked his immense length.

He smiled.

She creamed.

A strange banging sound ripped her from her erotic vision.

She blew out a tense breath. She needed to focus on her assignment, not fantasize about Jim.

The knocking sound continued. Was someone hitting on a door? Was someone locked in a room somewhere? Could it be an unwilling sex slave? Maybe the missing woman they were searching for?

On shaking legs, she quickly slipped on the negligee and crept into the dark hallway.

The banging sounds came from next door.

She tiptoed down the hall where she was surprised to find the door open. Peeking inside, her heart fluttered at the sight. Candles flickered everywhere and the scent of vanilla wafted beneath her nose. She squinted through the semi-darkness toward the noise and froze.

Oh-my-God.

A dark haired man, naked, his back toward Sky, was thrusting madly into the woman named Loren. She sat on some sort of wood chair, her legs clasped tight around the man's muscular hips, pressing kisses into his thick corded neck. With every powerful thrust, the back of the chair banged against the wall.

Before the woman could see her, Sky stole back into the hallway.

Did Loren know she was about to be sold to a mistress? Was the man fucking her some sort of going away present for herself?

She stopped short as something niggled at the back of her mind. That man. He seemed familiar. Although she'd only seen him from the backside...hadn't he looked a little like one of those "giggly boy" Sex Squad detectives Jim had scolded during briefing last week?

Sky shook her head. No way. Couldn't be him. The Chief had been adamant only two detectives would be filled in on this case.

Aside from risking another look into the room, or entering and tapping the guy on his shoulder asking to look at his face, she decided it wasn't him. She tiptoed further down the hallway.

At the next open doorway, she halted. Her pulse began to pound violently at the sight. This one also glittered with scented candles. The aroma was different. This one smelled of roses. Romantic roses.

Oh for heavens sakes, was she Alice in Wonderland and been dumped down the rabbit hole to enter a world or sex?

In the room, on the bed, sat four very attractive young people, their legs crossed. Two were women. Two were men.

She recognized the heart-shape faced woman with the auburn hair as Carmella. Loverboy's partner.

All four people were completely nude. And they were not at all embarrassed about being that way.

Gosh, she envied him. Why couldn't she be so bold with her nudity?

"My turn," Carmella laughed. She drew a card from the deck between them on the bed and read it. She smiled.

"Position 32. Climb on top of your partner and impale yourself."

Sex card game.

Carmella picked the cutest guy of the two. Grinning from ear to ear, the man stretched full length on the king sized bed. His penis stuck straight up in the air.

She held her breath and watched as Carmella crouched over the man and lowered herself onto his long penis. The woman grimaced as he disappeared inside her. Her loud hiss made Sky exhale softly as she creamed.

Unbelievable.

She wondered why Loverboy hadn't registered himself as a Sex Slave Trainer? Why was he avoiding paying his taxes? Could it simply be greed? Or maybe he was deceiving these young people? Perhaps he was telling them he could provide employment so they could be trained more easily? And then when they finished their training, he sold them into slavery and kept the money all to himself?

Sounded like a pretty good motive for tax evasion. But could she prove it?

Sky moved to the next door. It was open too. Didn't anyone value his or her privacy around her?

She peeked inside. The delicate scent of magnolias filled the air as scented candles flickered everywhere. This room was quiet. Movement in a far corner caught her attention and Sky's mouth dropped open when she spotted two naked men standing in the corner.

Both had their backs toward her. She couldn't help notice one of the men had the curviest, sexiest ass cheeks she'd ever seen. She breathed hard when she realized it was Loverboy and the other man was Jim.

Chapter Four

The spoke to each other in low voices, but not low enough that she couldn't make out what they were saying.

"Tonight you'll practice the trigasm on her." Loverboy said to Jim.

Trigasm? Sounded erotic.

Jim nodded. "I've studied up on it."

"Carmella said you were a quick study. I'm sure you won't disappoint your partner."

To her shock, both men suddenly turned around.

"Ah, Sky," Loverboy said. He didn't seem surprised to see her.

Jim, on the other hand, appeared angry. His mouth was set tight. His erection blossomed as he gazed daggers at her.

"I'm glad to see you are eager to get into the swing of things," Loverboy remarked.

Sky tried hard to act natural. To act as if this wasn't her first time standing in a sexy negligee in front of two men. She focused her mind on the four men and women she'd seen earlier sitting cross-legged on the bed. Focused on how casual they'd acted in the nude.

Sweet mercy, as hard as she tried, she couldn't keep her face from heating at Jim's hungry stare.

"There's that virgin blush, again." Loverboy cooed.

Beside him, Jim stiffened and quickly came to her rescue. She shivered at his icy tone. "This must be my partner. The one you were talking about."

Loverboy nodded. "Go easy on her. She's unsure whether she wants to become a sex slave. Give her a real good time, though."

"I intend on doing just that." Jim's gaze bored straight into hers until she averted her gaze.

"I'll be going." Loverboy said. "I have a few more students to check on. I'll pop in once in a while to see how things are going in here. If you'll excuse me."

When Loverboy left the room, Sky stood paralyzed as Jim continued to study her without saying a word. She gazed back at him, studying the wonderful expanse of shoulders that flowed out to bulging muscles in his arms. Muscles also ridged his narrow belly and abdomen. Tufts of dark hair grew across his broad chest and arrowed down...

Oh my!

His cock was very...erect.

A few more heartbeats of silence followed. Jim's gaze snapped to a corner of the room and quickly back to her. Instantly she knew he was indicating they were being watched. Before she had the time to even experience embarrassment, Jim began to walk toward her. She couldn't seem to keep her eyes off...*it*.

The anticipation of actually have his cock impaling her made a low moan escape her lips. She took a deep breath, drawing the warm scented air into her lungs and tried to relax. Couldn't.

She tried to think. Couldn't do that either. Gosh, Jim's penis was so huge. Excitement coursed through her. It weakened her, urged her to reach out to him...

No! She should stay away from him. But he looked so good without clothes.

"If I hadn't been here that bastard would be fucking you right now," he said in such a low voice she could barely hear her as he brushed past her.

"Any objections?" she teased.

He swore softly beneath his breath and shut the door with a slam, then he whirled around to face her.

"Why the hell are you walking around like this? You're just begging for a man to fuck you, aren't you?" he whispered.

"I thought you said I would be the one who couldn't handle this?"

He blinked at her as if she'd just slapped him.

"I can handle it, if you can." His voice had turned to a deadly calm. She didn't miss the note of challenge. For a moment she wanted to warn him that he was right and she had been drugged, but before she could voice her concern, he spoke again.

"Lay down on the bed. On your back. With your ass near the edge. Lift your knees up. Feet on the mattress. Spread your legs. You're about to be taught a lesson."

"Another finger fucking?" she asked, her breath hitching in her throat.

"How'd you know?"

Sweet heavens, how far were they going to take this? They were supposed to be searching for the missing woman. But they were also supposed to participate in Loverboy's world too, if necessary. In the way she craved a satisfying release, this lesson was necessary.

Heat shot through her as she slowly lay on the bed and did as he'd instructed. When she lifted her knees up and spread her legs, he walked toward her.

She swallowed at the hungry intensity in his brown eyes as his gaze caressed her body before settling on her pussy.

"Tonight's lesson is the trigasm," he said thickly.

Her breathing grew deeper, her breasts rose and fell in a sensuous rhythm. Her nipples had never felt so tight and achy. She wanted to tear the sheer cloth of the negligee from her body.

She inhaled sharply as he came around the side of the bed. He reached out and grabbed a pillow. He ordered her to raise her head and he placed the cushion beneath her neck. Then he grabbed another pillow.

"Lift your hips."

Her heart cracked against her chest as she did what he asked.

A moment later, the soft support was seated in such a way as her hips were high and her ass and pussy bared to him.

"Perfect," he commented. She watched him move to a nearby bureau.

"Now we just need some gloves." He snapped on a pair of latex gloves and then he grabbed a tube.

"Lots of lube required for this lesson."

Oh my!

He walked to the foot of her bed and she hissed as his palms branded her inner thighs and he pried her trembling legs open wider for his inspection. His masculine aroma reached her nostrils, the intoxicating of soap and male scent sent her heartbeat soaring.

"A trigasm can be achieved by vigorously massaging the three points of pleasure." The anger was slowly leaving his voice replaced by a sensuous tone.

"And what would those three be?" she whispered, obsessed with the need shining in his eyes.

His right hand slid slowly along her inner thigh leaving a trail of tingling heat. His fingers parted her pussy lips and his eyes widened with appreciation as he studied her reaction.

Sky held her breath with anticipation.

When his thick thumb pushed against her clit, she inhaled a moan and shivered. He moved his thumb over her sensitive clit in small, slow torturous circles, making her ache and gasp and buck her hips.

"Number one pleasure point is the clitoris," he rumbled. His thumb moved sensuously. His full lips were tight with concentration.

Her vaginal juices slurped as his fingers dipped inside her vagina and came out in a teasing promise of things to come. The creamy moistness between her thighs grew. His pace quickened. The pressure increased. Sky closed her eyes as the whirlwinds of pleasure ripped through her.

Sweet torture.

His thumb kept the pressure as it swirled against her clit. She cried out when a couple of his fingers slipped into her channel. About an inch inside, he pressed a finger along the wall of her vagina. Sky inhaled sharply at the gesture.

"Number two is the g-spot." Jim murmured. "It is the spongy area that can be felt through the front wall of the vagina."

"G-spot?" she gasped.

"It exists. I'll prove it to you."

The pressure of his fingers increased as he searched along her vaginal wall and his thumb continued to rub against her clit. She closed her eyes tighter, the tension in her mounted. Her fingers drew to her swollen breasts and she pinched her nipples.

She tossed her head back into the fluffy pillow and allowed the sweet torture to rule her body.

"The size and sensitivity of g-spots differ in women. In order to find it, I have to explore. Once I find it, I use the come-hither technique. It means I wave my finger," Jim's husky voice came from somewhere far away. His finger move slightly inside her, back and forth and Sky jerked as he touched a sensitive spot inside her vagina. She creamed really hard.

"Here it is. The key is to keep you aroused. Keep the touch firm."

As promised, he increased the pressure on her g-spot. Heated wetness poured from her vagina. Her thighs trembled uncontrollably. His movements against her clit were exquisite agony. One hand left her inner thigh and he reached for the tube he'd placed on the bed. He squeezed it, dabbed the lube onto his fingers and dropped the tube. The man was quite efficient with one hand, wasn't he?

He reached between her thighs and she bucked as a large lubed finger dipped inside her anal canal. The sensation was strange. Filling. Awesome pressure.

Sky shuddered at the intimate gesture.

"Third area for a trigasm is the anus."

Oh God! Her hips instinctively arched higher allowing him easier access to her. Liquid heat whipped along her vagina and she ached for him to mount her. To plunge into her. To quench this insane fire raging through her.

"Clitoris. G Spot. Anus," he whispered. His finger movements were now sensual and in perfect rhythm. She couldn't take it anymore. She needed release. Now!

"Jim! Please!"

"What?"

"Fuck me!" she gasped.

"I can't do that, Sky. Remember? You wanted to remain a virgin until we're married," he whispered.

Disappointment rippled along her excruciating sensations. She was going to go insane if he didn't bring her relief.

"Please," she begged.

His finger in her anus speared deeper. The fingers in her vagina withdrew and began to thrust hard.

An orgasm was coming. She could feel it. She whimpered with excitement.

"Faster! Oh God! Faster!" she urged.

The fingers impaling her vagina and ass thrust firmer. Became more violent. More frantic.

The pressure built to intolerable pleasure. Sky screamed. Hard and loud. She didn't care who heard her. She didn't care about anything except the incredible shudders wracking her as she convulsed and bucked into a wondrous pleasure land.

*****

Sky lay in front of him. Her breasts heaved sensuously as she breathed from the trigasm that had shaken her body. Her pussy was open and spasming, eager for him to enter. And boy did he want to enter. To bury his aching cock rod into her and take her to new heights. It's what he'd wanted for so long and she was giving him permission.

Yet, he couldn't do it. Until now, she'd stuck to her principles. She'd wanted to remain a virgin until she got married.

Shit! He wanted her so fucking bad his cock spasmed and jerked from the need. But it wasn't fair to take her when she was so goddamn vulnerable and drugged. For his saintly efforts of restraint, he was experiencing the worst hard on he'd ever had in his entire life.

When she opened her pretty blue eyes, his heart twisted at the love glittering for him. The trust and the need for release. Her want for more sex. The craving for his love. And he needed her in his life too. The realization made him curse softly.

Slowly her eyes widened as her gaze lowered to his erection. That sweet pink tongue popped out of her wet mouth as she licked her bottom lip.

Then she smiled. It was a challenging smile. It made Jim wonder what the hell she was up to.

On a moan, she sat up. As she scrambled on her hands and knees toward him, her breasts jiggled invitingly. When her face came level with his cock, her breath caressed his shaft.

Sweet Jesus! Was she about to do what he hoped?

His cock pulsed with need as she stared at it. Her beautiful face was serene as she opened her mouth. He grit his teeth as her moist, velvety lips curled around the tip of his hard cock.

Damn! The inexperienced way her mouth tightened around him made the need in his penis mount to a painful level. He staggered as his knees weakened from arousal and he curled his hands around her shoulders to steady himself.

"Suck!" he groaned.

Through half lidded eyes, he watched as her cheeks hollowed out and she sucked and slurped. Shards of lightning ripped through his shaft slamming into his balls and right into his gut. Her tongue moved sensuously along the underneath part of the head. The gesture made him cry out at the pleasure cascading up and down his trembling shaft.

He tensed as her tongue slithered around his head. His breathing grew labored. The heat of her moist mouth clamped around his rod was so damn good. How the hell could her innocent probing turn him on so much? He hadn't felt like this with even the most experienced women he'd been with.

Her lips loosened slightly and she took more of him inside her mouth. Her lips moved in slow, torturous actions that left him gasping. He groaned when her hands came up and covered his balls. The intimate gesture had his thighs quaking and he almost dropped to his knees. Her fingers explored his scrotum. She twisted and kneaded and made him groan. His hips thrust forward, slamming his penis deeper into her mouth.

He gyrated and hoped she wasn't frightened. His concerns were put to rest when her tongue seductively circled his stiff cockhead sending incredible jolts through his shaft. He thrust into her mouth and her lips stretched tight over his flesh, her mouth, a scorching cavern. So goddamn hot and wicked moist. He thrust faster.

A moan slipped from her mouth. To his surprise she took him in deeper. Her fingers stroked his balls. The pressure in his penis grew to an intolerable level.

"Sky!" he gasped. "I'm going to come!"

She didn't appear hear his warning. She slurped and licked the tip of his penis, encouraging him to spew. He thrust uncontrollably. Tangling his hands into her feathery hair, he then cupped the back of her head and pulled her face against him.

He thrust harder. Violently. A frenzy of sensations convulsed through his shaft. Her moist mouth made love to his fiery flesh. His breath caught in his lungs. His body tightened erotically and he couldn't hold back anymore.

He quaked and on a strangled moan, he ejaculated into her mouth. The release was magnificent. Her tight mouth continued to suck until he was dry and shuddering and weak from his release.

When she let go, he slumped onto his knees in front of her. She continued to stay in her position on her hands and knees on the bed as they stared at each other. Their gazes clashed as their breaths ripped through the air. Suddenly, her eyes darkened with desire.

What! She wanted him to give her another trigasm?

"Nice to see you two getting so acquainted," Loverboy's amused voice curled through the candle lit room.

Jim gazed up to find Loverboy standing beside the bed. A cocky grin was plastered on his goddamn face. His lust filled eyes caressed Sky who suddenly looked scared. Jim tensed and fought the urge to cover her from Loverboy's hungry gaze.

Man! They'd been so enthralled with each other; they hadn't even heard Loverboy enter the room. He noticed Sky tense as Loverboy ran a long finger along her smooth ass.

Jim was about to tell him to get his dirty hands off his woman when Sky shot him a warning look.

"Well, Sky? How was the trigasm? Did Jim do a fine job?"

To Jim's surprise, the fear vanished from her face and her lips upturned into a delightful smile.

"He was absolutely wonderful. Where do I sign up for this sex slave course?"

Her words stunned Jim.

The urge to slam his fist into Loverboy's nose was so strong and he physically had to bite his tongue to prevent himself from losing control. It was only when he drew blood from where his teeth sunk into his flesh and pain exploded that he was able to push aside some of his anger.

"I'd like to speak some more to you about this course. In private. If that's alright?" she asked Loverboy.

Was she freaking crazy?

"I can give you all the details in my office. Then there is a contract to sign."

"If I like what I hear, I'll be more than willing to sign the contract."

Loverboy nodded, apparently satisfied.

"How about I show you to my office?" he said.

Jim tensed as he awaited her answer.

"I feel business should be business and pleasure should be pleasure," Sky said. "And since your office is a business environment, I'd appreciate the return of my clothes."

Relief swept over Jim. But in the way Loverboy frowned, it appeared he didn't like her demand.

Good! That prick didn't deserve to gaze upon Sky the way he was doing. Didn't deserve to even look at her. He should never have allowed her to come here. Why the hell hadn't he just kidnapped her after he'd learned she'd taken this assignment?

He should have stashed her somewhere safe. Somewhere no other man could stare at her nakedness. No man except him.

"Very well, Sky." Loverboy broke into his thoughts. "You are correct. Business should be business. Your clothes are in this closet." He pointed to a nearby door and then returned his gaze to Jim.

"Jim, would you mind showing Sky to my office?"

"No problem."

"I'll see you downstairs in a few minutes." Loverboy said.

When he left, Sky exhaled beside him.

"That bastard!" Jim cursed quietly as he headed for the closet. He flung open the door and withdrew her flimsy blouse and the sexy skirt.

"Where's your goddamn underwear?" he asked when his searching showed up no other items.

"I didn't wear any."

"You didn't? What are you thinking?" His anger was making him see red.

"Sexy is what I'm thinking, Jim. That is the whole point in trying to get Loverboy's attention, remember?"

She grabbed her clothes and he watched her quickly shrug out of her negligee and then done that tight skirt, effectively concealing her pussy from his gaze. Her luscious breasts bounced wildly as she slipped on her blouse.

His cock hardened.

"What are you going to do inside the office? Just the two of you," he snapped.

"Are you jealous, Jim?" Her eyes glittered with excitement.

"Watch what you say, woman or I'll show you exactly how jealous I can be," he warned.

Before she could button her blouse, he reached out and grabbed her wrists, stopping her cold.

He craved to taste her nipples as he'd done earlier in her room. She read the intent in his eyes, because she tried to break free from his grasp. He didn't let go.

"No, don't go yet. I want to look at you," he said as he peered at her luscious breasts.

"Jim, he's downstairs waiting."

"I don't goddamn care. You're mine. You belong to me. You hear me?"

Surprise flashed across her face. Didn't she know how much he wanted her? Didn't she know he was a stupid jerk for breaking their engagement?

"It's over between us, Jim. You said so yourself. You couldn't wait." Her softly spoken words slammed into his gut and he almost doubled over from the harsh impact.

"I lied. I can wait." The truth of his words made her inhale sharply. "Don't let him touch you, Sky."

"I won't."

"Promise me."

"Trust me," she whispered. The warmth from her breath caressed his mouth and he wanted a taste of her full lips. Just one quick taste. He was about to lower his head, but her hands slammed onto his chest, stopping him cold.

"I have to go. Where's his office?"

"I'll show you,"

"No, I think it's better if we split up, before..."

Before he lost control and began to make love to her right here and now.

"Down the stairs. Turn left through the living room. The door beside the television set. I haven't been able to search his office yet."

"I'll see what I can do. While I'm in there you check around for Sally. Or try to find out where she is."

Jim nodded. It was time to put sex with his ex aside. Reluctantly, he released her and impatiently watched her button up her blouse.

"I don't know why you wore that flimsy thing. It leaves nothing to my imagination," he grumbled as he stared at her dark nipples popping against the white material.

"That's the idea."

She winked and slipped out the door.

*****

You're mine! *You belong to me*!

Jim's words rang through Sky's head as she tiptoed barefoot down the stairs.

Was Jim serious? Or was it just his sex crazed mind talking?

Did she dare to hope they'd get back together? If what they'd just shared was any indication how good they would be in bed...

Sky blew out a tense breath as she remembered how he'd turned her into a moaning, writhing bundle of desire. She wanted more of that pleasure. First though, she needed to do her job. Then they could get out of here and talk things over like two civilized adults and maybe pick up their plans of getting married?

The door to Loverboy's office stood open and light streamed out into the dark living room. No sound came from the room. Peeking inside, she was glad to see his office empty. Popping inside, she quietly closed the door behind her, turned around and surveyed the room. It was a typical office. One desk flooded with papers. A couple of swivel chairs. A filing cabinet.

She headed for the filing cabinet. If the missing woman had come back to Loverboy willingly, she might have signed a contract.

As quietly as possible, she glided the top drawer open and surveyed the folders. Accounts Payable. Bills. Expenses. Nothing giving any indication of contracts.

She slid the second drawer open and smiled. Bingo! Names. The Chief's daughter's last name was Green. In a flash, she sifted to the G section and found what she was searching for.

A contract in the name Sally Anne Green. She'd been sold to a man living in Alaska for five hundred thousand dollars. The contract wasn't signed. Sky's heart picked up speed.

Three hundred grand? Very interesting.

What did the unsigned contract mean? Had Sally been forced into slavery? A sound from outside caught her attention. Dropping the contract back into the folder, she quickly slid the drawer shut and plopped into the nearest chair.

A split second later, the door swung open and Loverboy walked in. Thankfully, he was dressed in a white shirt and casual slacks.

Sky exhaled slowly. If he'd shown up naked expecting to her to perform on him, she would have died on the spot.

"I'm sorry to keep you waiting. I had to attend to some pleasure."

Okay.

"Now. Let me explain how our sex slave classes work."

He sat down on the chair behind his desk and clasped his hands behind his head, looking very relaxed. She wished she could calm down; unfortunately, all she could think about was Jim and praying he would be careful.

"You would be expected to perform any sexual duties your master or mistress asks. Including performing on any of his or her friends. Would you be comfortable with that?"

"Performing on someone other than my master?"

Loverboy nodded.

"I would have to obey my master, wouldn't I? His word would be my command regardless of whether I like it." Damned if she would sleep with any other man than Jim.

"During my training course you will be exposed to all the basics of what a master or mistress will demand from you. It is the best way to sensitize yourself to your new world. There will be classes in oral sex, anal sex, threesomes, different positions, and other exciting courses. The last week would be in the Sex Dungeon."

"What's that?"

Loverboy unclasped his hand from behind his head and leaned forward. Excitement gleamed in his eyes.

"Actually that is where I just came from. Your final week is spent in the Sex Dungeon where you are forced to put into practice what you've learned here. We have potential masters and mistresses who come and try you out."

Mercy. His slave business was serious and she would enjoy bringing this guy to justice for evading his taxes.

"The masters and mistresses experiment with the students in the Dungeon. There is also opportunity for both the potential owner and slave final experience to see if they are compatible, before a contract is signed."

"What a unique idea." Sky replied.

"I thought so too when my partner came up with the idea. Oh and before I forget to mention it, the Sex Dungeon is also available to all the Sex Slave students, past, present or future who attend my course. You are free to go downstairs anytime to try out the male or female we have down there. It gives the students an idea of what will happen to them when they leave here. Sky tried hard not to stiffen at his words. Tried hard not to shiver as she imagined herself locked away in a dungeon, forced to have sex with Loverboy or a stranger.

"I can't wait to have you in there," he whispered.

Oh boy.

"I wouldn't mind having a tour of the Sex Dungeon," she said. Sally Green's contract wasn't signed and Loverboy had mentioned a woman was down there. The possibility existed she could be Sally.

"First let's discuss the contract, shall we?"

Oh yes, the contract.

He slid a desk drawer open, drew out a paper and placed it onto a cleared area on his desk.

"The contract explains more in detail of what is expected from you as well as the courses you would take. Of course before you begin the lessons I would have to give you a physical."

Sky froze. A cold sheen of perspiration swept over her forehead.

"A physical?"

"To see if you are healthy. A potential master or mistress will want access to it. I will do blood tests for sexual diseases. An internal exam. Routine stuff."

Internal exam? Oh God! How the hell was she going to get out of this one?

"Since you are so eager, we can do it right now. I have an adjoining room where I do the physicals, draw the blood, get the urine. I'll courier the items to the lab and I'll have the results in twenty-four hours. Then, if everything checks out, we begin the serious lessons. No more fooling around like you did with Jim upstairs."

Sky's heart thumped loudly in her ears.

There was no doubt in her mind he'd been watching what had been happening between her and Jim. Did he believe that she wanted to be a student? The thought of Loverboy's hands touching her body made her feel sick. But what else could she do? She couldn't make him suspicious by denying his request for a physical.

She drew in a ragged breath and tried to steady her nerves. She had no choice but to agree. She nodded and Loverboy smiled.

Chapter Five

Red-hot anger ripped through Jim as he gazed down at the woman lying naked on the bed. He'd found Sally Green and she was drugged to her eyeballs.

She'd grown into quite the woman since the last time he'd seen her three or four years ago. Back then she'd been in pig tails, wearing braces and tomboyish when she'd opened the door to her home. She'd said nothing to him as she'd quickly accepted the files his boss had requested for Jim to bring over while his boss recovered from gall bladder surgery. Then she'd slammed the door shut in his face.

Now Sally was long legged and very curvy. A natural beauty.

Her waist length blond hair was tangled with perspiration. Her face was chalk white. Full breasts rose and fell as she breathed heavily.

Her long legs were spread eagle. Her shaven pussy exposed. Her eyes were wide open. Fixed as she stared straight through him.

He closed his eyes against the sickening sight, and remembered how only minutes ago he had seen Loverboy come through the secret door in the kitchen. He must have been down here with her.

Earlier, while Jim had searched the empty kitchen, he'd been surprised to see a part of the northern side of the kitchen wall begin to slid sideways. Only his quick thinking had enabled him to slip undetected into the nearby broom closet. Through the crack in the slightly open door, he'd watched Loverboy turn the thermostat one full turn and the door swung shut.

Man! He wouldn't have believed it if he hadn't seen it. A secret door to an underground passage that led to several locked rooms. This one had been the only one unlocked. It appeared that Loverboy had been in too much of a hurry to get to his meeting with Sky.

Sally moaned, breaking him out of his thoughts. Her lashes fluttered and her sightless eyes closed. Jim reached down and lifted her limp arm. Her skin felt clammy and cool as he pressed two fingers against her wrist.

Her pulse was strong but slow.

"Sally? Sally? Can you hear me?"

"Loverboy? You back so soon? You just can't get enough of me, can you?"

She smiled and then opened her eyes. She giggled. She reached up and ran a finger along his jaw line.

"What did they give you, Sally? Do you know?" he asked.

Her brows pressed together in a frown. "Sex drugs. It's part of the course. You should know that."

She blinked, trying to focus.

"Who are you? You're not Loverboy."

"I'm a student here."

"Sent down to fuck me?"

Jim didn't say a word as he tried to figure out how in the world he was going to be able to get her out of here in her present condition.

Without warning, she reached out and grabbed him around his waist, holding so tight, he couldn't get away.

"Do with me what you want. Your wish is my command, master," she said as she gazed up at him.

Her head lolled sideways like a rag doll. She giggled again.

Oh great. Jim scanned the room searching for her clothing. He saw nothing. Not even a goddamn bed sheet to cover her nakedness.

"I'm here to get you out, Sally."

"I'm not leaving here. I'm almost finished my course." Her smile widened. "I'm pretty sure that big man will take me. He had no trouble sticking his big cock into my ass. I told Loverboy I want him. Or maybe I'll take you. You're cute."

Her grasp around his waist tightened.

To his shock, she pressed a hot kiss against the head of his semi-erect penis.

Jesus. He needed to find clothes for both of them and then he had to get her out of here. Fast.

"Sorry Sally, I'm already taken."

"I should have known Loverboy would find someone for you. How come I haven't seen you here before?"

Her eyes narrowed with curiosity.

"Haven't we met before?"

"I'm new." No use reminding her they'd met once several years ago at her parent's home. If she figured it out, his cover was blown.

"New? And you already have a mistress?"

"A girlfriend. Now c'mon, let's get you out of here. Your father is worried about you."

Sally blinked in puzzlement. Then she laughed.

"My father? Worried about me? Hell, he probably misses fucking me."

What the hell?

"Oh! Didn't daddy dearest tell you? I've been his sex toy since I was eight. I refuse to do it for free anymore. Tell my father he can go fuck himself! I'm not going back to him."

Great! Just great! What the hell was he supposed to do now? Believe what she was telling him? It could be the drugs talking, but from the pain flashing in her eyes, she was making a believer out of him that she could be telling the truth.

Should he still try to get her out of here? Or leave her to her fate?

"Why you go to the cops and implicate Loverboy?" he asked.

"I never went to the goddamn authorities. My father made it up when I told him I wanted to be a sex slave. My only mistake was throwing it in his face that I was being trained by Loverboy."

Jim inhaled in frustration. This whole assignment was just a ruse brought up by a jilted father?

He gazed down at Sally and at the way her eyes were fixed because of the sex drugs. Drugs that she was fully aware of and fully accepting.

Who the hell was he to make the decision of what Sally Green should do anyway? She was eighteen. Legal age to do whatever she wanted.

A faint puff of alluring perfume sunk a warning to Jim. Someone else was in the room along with himself and Sally. He recognized the scent and he grew cold. Carmella's perfume.

Sally's grip around his waist tightened. A noise erupted from immediately behind him and before he could wrench himself free from Sally's hold, pain exploded like a bomb against the right side of his head. The impact stunned him. Bright white stars blinded his vision.

He blinked. The stars remained. The ground came up to meet his face. He groaned as someone kicked at his legs. He wanted to kick back. Nothing happened.

Rough hands grabbed his shoulder and rolled him onto his back. The stars danced wildly, making him nauseous. Carmella's perfume drove deep into his lungs.

"He's the undercover cop I was telling you about. Want me to kill him?" a man said.

Jim's blood chilled in his veins. That man's voice was unmistakable. He was one of Jim's Sex Squad detectives. A man with a perfect work record who'd asked for a position on the Squad. He was one of the two men who hadn't taken the Loverboy case seriously enough during Briefing last week. Or at least Jim had thought he hadn't taken it seriously. Apparently, he had, because here he was.

"No, Loverboy wants him alive," Carmella replied.

Someone lifted his feet. Hands slid under his armpits. He was being lifted and the room whirled violently. Before he blacked out he could only think of Sky, and how he should never have walked out on her.

*****

"Sky. There's no need to be frightened." Loverboy drawled.

Damn, he could see right through her.

"It's just a physical," he said as he slipped on a pair of latex gloves while he stood beside the cot he'd instructed her to lay on. "I won't hurt you. I just need to feel around inside. It's the same as a pap smear."

"I'm not afraid," she replied as she slid off the cot. "I guess I'm a little shy. I need just a little more time. A day or two."

Loverboy frowned. "You didn't seem shy with Jim."

"Oh, well, he's a fellow student."

Lame excuse.

"Meaning?"

Her cheeks burned with embarrassment.

"I'm attracted to you. It wouldn't be professional. I'd enjoy your touch." She lied. Sickness clawed at her belly at the thought of him touching her.

"All the more why I should touch you, Sky. I can pleasure you in ways you've never dreamed of."

He started toward her.

Oh dear. She was in trouble here. Jim, where the hell are you?

"I thought you didn't do virgins?" she stammered as she walked to the other side of the cot putting it between them.

"I lied."

Big news flash there.

"Virgins are my weakness," Loverboy cooed as he slowly trailed her. His eyes burned with lust.

"How's that?" she asked. She rushed through the adjoining door into his office and circled behind his desk, stalling for time. If she could keep him talking, she might be able to get to the other door.

"My upbringing. The nuns where I had to stay were virgins until they forced me to service them."

Sky blinked in disbelief.

"They fucked me." Anger coiled in his voice. "In the orphanage they ran. I protested at first. But they were women. Lonely women. Bigger than me. Stronger. I found out quickly they were sensuous creatures who only wanted to be loved. They weren't meant to be locked away in a convent without the love of a man. So, they used us orphanage boys. I serviced the nuns for years. Even while I was a preacher. I learned to look for the yearning in their eyes. But you're different, Sky. I saw the yearning in your eyes. The yearning for a man you'd lost. He hurt you so bad. He made you vulnerable. Despite that fact, there's a strength in you I just can't help but to try to dominate. I couldn't leave you in that bar to get fucked by some stranger. I want you all to myself."

"If you love to fuck women, why bother becoming a preacher?"

His eyes glazed over with remembrance. Sky poised herself ready to run for the door.

"I did it for the nuns. They thought if I became a preacher I'd stay with them."

Okay, this guy was nuts. His whole background was loony.

"And you could forgive them for their carnal sins during confession? I bet they thought you would be the closest thing to making love to God, am I right?"

His eyes twinkled with amusement.

Sweet heavens, he actually thought she was serious?

"Actually, yes. You're right."

She needed to get out of here. Now!

She dashed toward the door. Her back prickled in warning and she screamed as Loverboy's strong hands curled around her waist.

*****

Damn, his head hurt like a son of a bitch. The last thing he remembered was Sally Green holding him around his waist. And Carmella's perfume. Then excruciating pain as someone bashed him over his head. And his cover being blown by one of his own Sex Squad team members.

He tensed and opened his eyes.

Directly above him was a thick beamed ceiling with a lit bare light bulb. The air smelled musty. Damp. They must have dumped him in one of those other rooms in the basement. He tried to turn his head to get a better view of his surroundings, but something had been strapped over his forehead, preventing movement. Panic hummed along his nerves.

He smelled leather. Leather restraints.

A band was across his forehead. Another velvety strap pinned down his neck.

He tested his arms. Restraints pinned his elbows and his wrists. He noted his arms stretched outward at ninety-degree angles. He wiggled his fingers. At least something was free. It gave him a glimmer of hope.

Mentally he checked the rest of his body. His legs were spread-eagle. Bands lashed over his knees and ankles. Everything was secure.

He lifted his hips up and then down, gasping at the sharp needle pricks of pain biting into his ass cheeks. What the hell? He repeated the maneuver.

When he lowered his ass, this time ever so gently, the same thing happened.

Ouch.

Okay. So he was supposed to keep his ass still. He could do that.

He was totally defenseless. And totally naked.

Great. Just great.

What the hell did they plan on doing to him down here? Were they going to turn him into one of those sex slaves? Pump drugs into him like they'd done to Sally Green?

Making love to strange women wasn't his cup of tea. He wanted only one. Sky. And now that he'd experienced the sexual side of her, he wanted her in his life even more.

A soft sexy moan drifted to his ears. A woman's moan. A man's grunt.

The light bulb overhead swayed slightly. Mattress springs creaked making Jim's pulse begin to hammer.

Was the moaning woman, Sky? Was Loverboy fucking her?

White-hot anger flared.

The moans grew louder. They didn't sound like Sky. Her moans had been distinct. Sweet and sexy and innocent.

This had to be someone else. Maybe his kidnappers?

Jim rolled his eyes. His kidnappers could be having sex right over his head. More grunts and moans followed. Whoever was up there was certainly going at it. Good and hard.

The stairs creaked and he held his breath. Someone was coming down the stairwell. He winced at the sound of a heavy bolt screeching across a metal door. A key grated in the lock.

Having him trussed like a Thanksgiving turkey and held under lock and key meant they didn't want him going anywhere. His heart cracked against his chest as the door opened. Footsteps echoed as someone entered the room.

Carmella hovered into view. Shit! He couldn't deny she was a beautiful woman. He'd had a hell of time getting her attention when he'd started to frequent the Sexy Toys Shop she owned, but to his surprise she'd invited him to the farmhouse. He should have known he was being set up, but he'd been blind with worry for Sky and a chance that she may not have backup. So he'd done a few things he was ashamed of doing like participating in a couple of those lessons, before Sky had turned up. Hell, truth was, he would have done anything to get into Loverboy's slave course to be Sky's backup.

Carmella blinked down at him. Soft brown curls caressed her heart shaped face. Her full mouth pouted sexily.

"I'm glad to see you're awake." Her voice sounded soft and delicate and deadly.

He flinched as her soft fingers caressed what he suspected was a goose egg sized lump just above his temple where pain radiated.

"I see I hit you a little too hard. I do apologize, Jim."

"What's the big idea strapping me down like this, Carmella?"

"Just relax. Let me massage away your headache."

He wanted to protest but when her fingers began massaging his temple with tiny, gentle soothing circles, the pain ebbed away almost immediately. It appeared she was an expert on whacking people and bringing relief.

Despite the tenseness of the situation, he calmed under her ministrations. With the relaxation came curiosity.

His gaze dropped from her pretty face and followed the slender column of her neck to the curve of her shoulder. A very naked shoulder with a dusting of rust colored freckles. He followed the trail of freckles down to...

She was naked. Not good.

Two very large breasts jiggled not too far away from his mouth. Dusky rose nipples poked straight out at him as if to say, here I am, have yourself a taste.

He swallowed nervously. He didn't know why he should be so surprised to see her nude. He'd seen her naked as he'd watched her entertain the students during lessons over the past couple of nights since arriving here.

"What do you want, Carmella?"

The tip of her tongue peeked through her slightly parted lips and her hopeful gaze raked down to his penis. "You are very well endowed."

"I've no complaints so far."

"Most women say size matters. I tend to agree with them, but the man must know what to do with his hands, mouth and cock, in order to bring about the utmost pleasure in a woman."

Suspicion whipped through him.

"Exactly what kind of game are you playing?"

"Curious, mia cara? That's wonderful. It means you're open to new and exciting things."

"Listen, if you're searching for a fascinating fuck, I can oblige you. Just untie me." *Then I'll leave*, he added silently. There was no way he'd let this woman introduce him to "new and exciting".

"I don't want to untie you, darling. I prefer a...captive audience." Lust sparkled in her eyes.

He swallowed nervously. He needed to get out of here. Pronto.

"Carmella? What are you planning to do to me?"

"Please don't be frightened, Jim."

A shiver of fear crawled up his spine. Past experience had taught him to be scared when someone told him not to be. His breath caught as a warm fingertip pressed delicately against his lips.

"Shh." Her finger began to massage the left corner of his mouth with soothing little circles like she'd done to his temple. Slowly. Gently. Erotically.

The corner of his mouth began to loosen. She switched to his other side and she massaged until the tightness evaporated.

What was she up to?

"It won't work," he growled, getting pissed off at being a captive.

"What won't work, darling?"

"Whatever you are trying to get me to do. It just won't work."

"What is it I'm trying to do?" she asked sweetly.

"You're trying to seduce my mouth into doing something for you. I'm not playing your games, Carmella. I'm a new student here. I haven't been introduced to all the new exciting things yet. Why don't we wait until I'm more...experienced?"

"Jim, you're way too experienced for this place. You are after all, a Sex Squad detective."

"Quit the crap, Carmella. What are you planning to do with me?"

She pouted. "Oh pooh, you Sex Squad detectives need so much work in loosening you up. I can see you aren't interested in playing with me tonight. But there is something I do have to tell you before I release you..."

Jim frowned. The coolness in her voice told him she was about reveal something he wasn't going to like.

*****

"Don't be frightened, Sky." Loverboy said as she struggled in his arms.

"Frightened? Me?" She tried to laugh. Couldn't. "I'll show you how scared I am. Would you care to join me in my bedroom?"

Hopefully at the invitation, Loverboy would let go of her and she could escape. To her relief his grip loosened slightly.

"I'd prefer to do you right here, Sky. Right here on the cot. Except I won't make love to you with my fingers, like Jim did at Sex Squad Headquarters."

Sky froze.

Loverboy chuckled.

"Oh come on! Don't look so surprised, Sky Kelley, Sex Squad Detective. You honestly think I don't keep track of my incoming virgins?"

"You better be careful, Loverboy." Sky warned. "I am a government agent. People know I'm here. It can get quite sticky if I should disappear."

"Oh Sky, ye of little faith. Nothing's going to happen to you. That is, nothing that you don't want to happen."

Sky swallowed, her throat suddenly went dry.

"What do you mean?"

"It means we're going up to your room, Sky."

Dread grabbed hold of her. There was no way in hell she was going to have sex with Loverboy. No way in hell!

On the other hand...The cuffs! She had handcuffs stuffed in a secret compartment in the lining of her purse. The purse was in her room. But she didn't remember seeing it when she'd searched for her clothes. Panic welled again.

No! Wait a minute. She'd left her purse in the bathroom. By the sink. They might have missed it when they'd taken her clothes. She'd already had a fictional story ready too in case the cuffs had been discovered. She enjoyed bondage.

"Let's head up to your room, Sky. Nice and slow. No funny moves. When we get there, if you'd like we can have drinks and I can slip something in, like in the bar."

Jim had been right!

She could scream. She should have done so already, but she'd never been the screaming type. Now would be a good time to change that.

As if sensing what she was about to do, his hand clamped over her mouth.

"I don't want my students disturbed, Sky. Not that they would come to your aid anyways". His palm remained over her mouth and his arm stayed snug around her waist as he led her from his office. They entered the dark living room.

Frantic, she searched for Jim. He was nowhere in sight.

As they ascended the stairs, her mind tumbled with escape ideas. The thought of pushing herself backward against Loverboy was foremost. One swift shove would send him falling. But with the tight grip around her waist, she'd roll down with him. Her best bet lay with the handcuffs.

At the top of the stairs, her legs wobbled as she poised to break loose when Jim jumped out to her rescue. Nothing happened. A drop of perspiration dribbled down the side of her face. Another one dripped down her back.

The hallway was long. The longest hallway she'd ever walked down in her life. She didn't know how she managed to keep herself together. Didn't know how she didn't bolt and run.

As she passed the open doorways, men's groans and women's sensual whimpers mingled with creaking bedsprings. Fear encased her, making her only thought of escaping Loverboy, finding Jim and getting the hell out of here.

When they reached her room, Sky stopped in the doorway and blinked in shock.

Candles flickered everywhere. The distinct scent of lilac permeated the air. Filling her room with candles meant only one thing. He meant to have sex with her.

Chapter Six

Terror at the prospect of an attack made her dizzy. Her insides shook. Her legs wobbled like jelly. The door closed behind them and Loverboy uncapped her mouth but he didn't let go of her waist.

"No screams, Sky. You don't want any harm to come to Jim do you?"

Instinctively she knew his cover was blown too.

"What have you done to him?"

"He's...tied up at the moment, but you'll see him shortly. I promise."

She needed to get to the cuffs. Now!

"I have to use the bathroom," she said tightly.

"I'll accompany you."

"I...I can go myself."

"No," Loverboy said firmly.

He walked her into the bathroom. Her anxiety mounted when from the candlelight flickering through the open doorway she spied her purse on the countertop, exactly where she'd left it.

"I have protection in my purse," she said as she reached out and grabbed it.

He yanked the purse out of her hand. Sky almost screamed in frustration.

"Go. Now."

"I don't have to go anymore," she whimpered.

He grunted angrily and led her back into to the bedroom.

A moment later, he began nuzzling her neck, his free hand sliding up and down her arm in a caressing gesture.

"You don't have to be afraid of me, Sky," he whispered.

Her heart cracked like a whip as she frantically tried to figure out her next move. Jim was in trouble and she had to find out where he was. Looking down, she noticed he'd dropped the purse onto the night table. The purse was angled in such a way that she was able to dip her hand into the side pocket and rip the special tear-away material of the secret lining. A split second later, her fingers slid onto the cold metal of the handcuffs.

Loverboy's warm breath sizzled across the back of her neck, tickling the fine neck hairs. He pressed his lips against her skin. Fear wrapped around her body making her legs tremble. She would have to act very fast if she was going to get out of this mess.

She managed to slip the cuff around his wrist and readied to snap it shut when Loverboy suddenly pushed her. In a flash, she lost her balance and flopped onto her back upon the bed. She gasped in surprise when Loverboy grabbed both her wrists, swung her arms over her head and in a second he snapped a cuff over one wrist. He then slid the cuff around a wagon wheel spindle in the headboard and cuffed her other wrist. She was effectively secured to the bed.

"You son of a bitch!" Sky shouted. She tried to bring down her arms but pain ripped through her wrists as the cuffs dug into her tender flesh.

"Please relax, Sky."

"Oh, I'll relax. When you're in a court of law brought up on kidnapping a government agent."

"Easy, honey. I already told you. I'm not going to hurt you."

"And the cuffs are just toys!" She spat.

He frowned.

"What else am I supposed to do when you attack me with them?"

Sky exhaled in frustration. "What are you planning to do to me?"

"Talk," he replied.

"About?"

"Sally Green."

"I saw Sally Green's Contract. You sold her for five hundred thousand dollars. You promise your slaves three hundred thousand. You're worse than the government. What you're doing is illegal, Loverboy."

"The rest of it is my finder's fee. I can offer you the same deal. That's more than you make in four years, isn't it? I can make you an expert at pleasing others and how to get someone to please you."

"I'm not for sale, Loverboy."

Loverboy grimaced and shook his head. "No, you're not. You want to get married. Live that old-fashioned dream about raising kids in a two-story house with a big backyard and a white picket fence. That's where Sex Squad Detective Jim McBride comes in."

Sky bit her bottom lip as her darkest fear engulfed her. Loverboy did have Jim. That's why he hadn't come to her rescue.

"Where is he?" she snapped and yanked angrily at her restraints.

His gaze softened. "He is being prepared."

"Prepared for what?"

"For your marriage, of course."

Had Loverboy gone nuts?

"I'm a preacher, Sky. You want to marry, Jim. He obviously loves you. I plan to proceed over the ceremony. As you know, marriage on Saturna requires the preacher to view the consummation. It's the law and then we'll leave you two to your honeymoon."

"Why?"

"Why what?"

"Why are you forcing us to get married?"

"Forcing you? No one is forcing you, Sky. You don't have to marry him. But it might be in your best interest if you two got hitched and displayed a united front. I'll be doing you a favor as husband and wife cannot testify against each other."

"What's that supposed to mean?"

Loverboy smirked.

"It means what Jim did to you at Sex Squad Headquarters is illegal, Sky. Sex on the job, is illegal. You were taped there and you were taped here. I have the tapes. If the Chief's superiors saw them you would lose your jobs and you'd be reprimanded and given stiff prison sentences."

"The Chief gave us his blessing to have sex if we needed to get your attention."

"I'm sorry Sky, but according to the revised assignment records on file, you weren't supposed to have sex."

Sky swore inwardly.

The smugness on Loverboy's face meant he'd obviously fixed everything in his favor. His next words confirmed her suspicions.

"As far as Sex Squad Headquarters is concerned, Sally Green never went missing . The Chief never gave you the go ahead to engage in sexual activities. A little behind the scenes face to face persuasion about what he was engaging in with his daughter has made him forget a few things that would have saved your asses. Your assignment was to merely infiltrate my farmhouse to check if I was training sex slaves illegally and get out with the information. No sex."

"You bastard! You paid someone off. Who's your contact?"

"You and Jim and the Chief are our contacts, of course. At least that's what will come out if you chose to tell anyone what transpired here." He withdrew an envelope from his back pocket. From it he dug a slip of paper and shoved it before her eyes.

Sky's blood ran cold as she read it.

"And for all your help in keeping quiet about my dealings in the sex slave industry, here's a wire transfer, Sky. To prove you are on my payroll. It is for $500,000 dollars placed in your account. There's one for Jim too. You say anything to anyone and this bribe will become public knowledge."

"You can't buy my silence."

He grinned smugly. "I already have."

This cannot be happening!

"You won't get away with this, Loverboy. I spoke directly to the Chief to get this assignment."

"As I said, the Chief will deny giving you permission for sexual encounters."

"Like hell he will."

"It's all been arranged, Sky. The Chief's daughter, Sally, is training in my farmhouse willingly. She wants to be a sex slave, but not for her father. If word gets out what he's been doing to her since she was young, he'd be joining you and Jim in prison. He has every reason to keep his mouth shut. So, do you and Jim."

"You're disgusting. The Chief would never do anything to hurt his only daughter. He loves her."

"He fucks her!" Loverboy spat angrily.

"You're a liar!"

"He's telling you the truth, Sky." Jim's bitter voice curled into the room. He stood in the doorway. Anger brewed in his eyes, but relief rushed through her to know he was okay.

"Jim! Thank God you're all right."

"Take the cuffs off her." Jim demanded as he walked into the room. She noticed Carmella standing in the doorway, a gun trained on Jim.

"I have the key. We keep them on, Jim," Loverboy stated. "The wedding will be more exciting this way."

Jim didn't appear to be surprised about a wedding. He'd obviously been told already about it.

The bed moved slightly as he sat down and smiled at her. The smile lit up his eyes to the point they twinkled with unmistakable love for her. Happiness and warmth filled her, despite the trouble they were in. Joy that he still cared deeply for her even after the fight they'd had last week.

"I'm so glad you're all right," he whispered.

"Nothing what getting out of these handcuffs won't cure."

He reached out and caressed her shackled wrists.

"Did he tell you?" She didn't know why she was whispering. Loverboy stood right behind Jim within hearing distance.

"About us getting married? Sally Green? The tapes he has on us? Or the substantial amounts of money he's stashed in our accounts?"

"I guess you know everything."

He nodded.

"Carmella told me. He set us up. A damn good job of it too."

"Why, thank you." Loverboy cooed from behind Jim.

Jim threw Loverboy a cold glare that made him shut up.

"Is it really true about Sally?" Sky whispered. "About the Chief abusing her since she was young?"

"I'm afraid so. I talked to her in the Sex Dungeon. She doesn't want anything to do with her father. She's made her decision. She wants to be a slave. She is of age. She is here of her own free will. There's nothing we can do."

"Shall we get on with the ceremony?" Loverboy interjected.

Jim stopped caressing her sore wrists and captured her gaze.

"Do you still want to marry me, Sky?" His voice was filled with hope and his nearness made her believe everything was going to be all right.

"With Loverboy watching us?" This was so not how she'd expected her marriage to begin, but what choice did they have? Laws both here and on Earth existed that the preacher plus family and friends, if they were available, watched the consummation of the marriage. She'd always been prepared for an audience at her wedding consummation, just not Loverboy.

Besides, Loverboy had set them up. If they didn't do as he said, then he would release the information about the money in bank accounts that were in their names. The sex tapes he said he had, of which she had no doubt he spoke the truth, would be released and they would go to prison. They were at Loverboy's mercy.

"If it isn't him, it'll be another preacher. I want to marry you, Sky. But I will wait if that's what you want."

"No."

Jim's sharp inhalation and the shocked expression on his face made her realize he'd misunderstood her.

"I mean no, we need to do what he says. Besides, I can't wait for you. Let's get married."

He grinned and his voice lowered so only the two of them were sure to hear.

"I'll give him a show that will make him so jealous, he'll wish he was marrying you instead of being the preacher."

An excited giggle escaped her lips.

Jim let go of her wrists and turned to Loverboy.

"Marry us. After you're finished, we want nothing more to do with you. Do you hear me? We'll keep quiet about your goddamn slave course and about Sally. But only because I want Sky protected. If it was only me in this, I'd be hanging your ass out to dry to anyone who'd listen."

Loverboy was smart enough not to say anything. The smugness zipped away from his face leaving him pale and shaken. He realized he was lucky to get off this easily.

Jim twisted back around to face her. He smiled with reassurance. It was a sexy smile. A teasing promise of things to come and her heart floated wildly in her chest.

"Look into my eyes, Sky. Pretend it's just us two."

She did as he said.

Love burned so intensely in his eyes she swore he'd never loved her more than at this exact moment. His brown gaze drew the breath from her lungs and she drowned in his unique masculine scent. The thought of what would soon be happening between them made her breasts tingle. Moisture wept from her vagina as her body began to ready for him.

Mild air whispered over her skin as he slowly peeled her tight skirt down and off her legs. Instinctively Sky spread her legs, allowing Jim to gaze upon her moist pussy. His eyes darkened to ravishing hunger.

He reached for the buttons on her blouse; his fingers trembled as they unbuttoned. Within seconds, he pushed the flimsy material aside, fully exposing her breasts. The mild air caressed her skin and made her nipples pucker to attention.

She'd been invited to many weddings in her life. She'd watched the groom make love to the bride in front of the preacher and all their family and friends as required by law. But never had she seen such intense love in their eyes as what flared in Jim's eyes as he gazed upon her now.

When she thought of those other weddings, a tinge of regret zipped through her. She'd wanted her friends to see how much she loved Jim. She'd wanted everyone to hear her screams of passion as he made her orgasm. She wanted them to witness Jim sinking his cock into her as they consummated their marriage.

Instead, she had Loverboy and Carmella as her witnesses. It would be a bittersweet wedding. But in the end, she did have Jim. And that's all that really mattered.

"You may begin to arouse the bride-to-be." Loverboy said. His tone was now strictly professional. The lust gone from his face. He was simply a preacher presiding over their wedding.

Loverboy's words were all the encouragement Jim needed. Reaching out he cupped her heavy breasts in his hot hands. He lifted them slightly as if to check their weight. It was an intimate gesture that made her breathing hitch and pick up speed.

"You're so beautiful," he whispered. "So damn beautiful."

Fire lanced through her at his tender words. She whimpered as he gently squeezed her breasts. His thumbs arched upwards, caressing her nipples. They were highly sensitive to his touch and Sky bit her lower lip to prevent from crying out. He continued this action until her breathing grew erratic and arousal soared. Then, he squeezed and plucked her nipples from their root to their sensitized tips.

Sweet agony whipped through her vagina. She ached and creamed with need, pulling against the cuffs, which held her wrists. She wanted to reach out, grasp his stiff cock, and guide it into her. The intensity to be filled by him, had her desperate.

"Now, Jim," she hissed.

"Not yet, Sky," he whispered gently. "I want to taste you. I want to love you."

His words were music to her ears.

"I love you so much," she whispered back. She ached for him. Wished they'd never fought. She shouldn't have been so defiant. But she wasn't one for giving into demands. He would have to get used to that. It seemed he already had or he wouldn't want to get married.

His fingers raked her sensitive nipples and she cried out as every nerve ending breathed fire. She arched against the tremors, wanting more of this fierce enjoyment.

Jim's cock slapped thickly against the inside of her thighs as he moved closer.

Sky cried out as his head lowered and his warm mouth covered a hard nipple, drawing it into his heated mouth. He expertly licked her plump nipples with his tongue. Nibbled with the tips of his teeth. Mind-blowing sensations shivered through her.

All sane thoughts burned as they hit the flames of the nearby candles. She moaned and writhed as he licked at her with unrestrained longing. The fire in her lower belly increased and consumed her. She gasped at the intensity. Shuddered as Jim feasted on her breasts like a man dining on his last supper.

And then he sucked. Hard. So hard her hips flew up off the bed and the tip of his hard rod touched her clit. Lightning ripped through her making her cry out. His mouth left her breast, leaving her nipple wet and wanting. The bed moved and she opened her eyes just in time to see his head lower to hers.

His mouth settled firmly over her lips encasing hers with his steely warmth. His full lips slid over hers like a sizzling invitation. His lips made love to hers before his moist tongue moved roughly into her mouth. Their tongues clashed. She moaned at the sensual impact. He backed off, allowing her access to his moist cavern. He tasted delicious.

But in seconds he tore his mouth away from hers, and awareness zipped along her nerve fibers as the mattress dipped beneath her. He was getting ready. It was time.

Her heart thumped madly. Sky jolted as his hands seared the inside of her thighs widening her legs even more.

Loverboy picked up the cue and cleared his throat.

"We are gathered here today to witness the joining of these two lovebirds."

Loverboy's voice faded away as Jim's hands slid under her butt and cupped her ass cheeks. Deep pleasure sunk wherever he touched. He lifted her hips and dipped his head between her legs. His hot breath blew onto her pussy making her thighs tremble. The bristle from his unshaven face seared her sensitive skin.

Sky cried out as his lips kissed her swollen wet flesh. His tongue pushed aside her pussy lips and he licked her clit. Her breathing quickened and grew shallow as Jim's hard tongue circled her clit of nerves. Circling and caressing then circling again.

Her lust rose to fever pitch. Her body pulsed and hummed. When Jim's long tongue skillfully slid into her vagina, Sky's brain short circuited and her hips convulsed at the unexpected onslaught.

Sweet God above! She was spiraling out of control.

His tongue dashed upward inside her, stopping to stroke her pleasure spot an inch or so inside her. Her vagina muscles convulsed and instinctively she wrapped her legs around his head, pulling him closer.

His tongue stroked in and out and she inhaled at the fantastic tension. She loved the way her vaginal muscles contracted around his tongue. Loved the way Jim sucked on her clit. Pressure mounted and she exploded. Waves of pleasure wrenched through her. Feverish spasms wracked her making her body jerk wildly.

She rocked her pussy onto his face, her slick heat slipping into his mouth. She sucked in ragged breaths as the pleasure spilled through her, carrying her away. When she finally stilled, she reluctantly unclasped her legs from around Jim's head. He withdrew his tongue and lifted his head, licking his lips greedily.

His face was flushed. A cocky smile tilted his lips.

"Damn you taste good."

Sky's heart burst with love.

"Jim, I never knew it could be so...wonderful," she whispered.

His eyes darkened and sweet arousal once again sprang to life deep in her belly.

His hands still cradled her ass and Sky suddenly realized she couldn't get enough of sex with Jim.

"More, please give me more," she begged.

Her eyes fixed on Jim's massive cock. He appeared hard. He must ache terribly. Despite his discomfort, he'd taken care of her needs, instead of his. She needed to bring him relief. Bring both of them relief. Needed to bury him inside her.

She made a grab for his cock but the handcuffs bit painfully into her wrists, reminding her where they were and what was happening. The denial of reaching out to him only increased her arousal.

"You're lucky I'm tied down or I'd return the favor and send you into convulsions," she chuckled.

"Promises, promises," he whispered back.

In the background, Preacher Loverboy cleared his throat and said rather quickly, "Do you Jim McBride, take Sky Kelley to be your lawfully wedded wife, in sickness and in health, for richer for poorer, until death do you part?"

Jim gazed directly into Sky's eyes. The dark sexy look shining in those brown depths made her heart pound harder.

"I do," he said in a strong, firm voice.

Happiness crushed Sky and tears slid over her warm cheeks.

"Sky Kelley," The preacher continued. "Do you take Jim McBride to be your lawfully wedded husband? In sickness and in health, for richer, for poorer, until death do you part?

"I do," Sky whispered.

Jim smiled proudly. Pure love brewed in his eyes. Love, excitement and fiery passion.

When Jim climbed into position between her legs, Sky shivered with eagerness. His swollen cockhead pressed teasingly into her opening and she held her breath with anticipation.

She wished he'd just plunge into her and satisfy that deep ache inside her. But he couldn't. Not yet. But soon.

"The ring?" Loverboy asked.

"Here," Jim awkwardly pried the ring off his little finger.

Sky couldn't help but to giggle. Where had he gotten the ring on such short notice?

"Place it on her finger."

Jim did as he was instructed. The ring fit perfectly.

"By the power invested in me, I now pronounce you husband and wife. You may consummate the marriage."

"I love you." Jim whispered and then with one violent thrust his large swollen cock thrust into her pussy.

Sky cried out as virginal pain shot through her, but Jim's mouth fused perfectly over hers cutting off the rest of her scream. Thankfully, the pain faded quickly into memory and his impalement stopped. His mouth moved over hers with an erotic sweetness that made her tremble.

Suddenly, he sank deeper into her. His shaft was long and thick and he opened her pussy wide, stretching her vaginal muscles.

God! He was huge. His erection was endless as he continued to fill her. Finally, she had taken all of him inside her and he stopped.

"You like?" he asked as he broke his mouth from hers.

Sky moaned in answer. She couldn't have spoken if her life depended on it. His impalement was insanely wonderful as he pulsed inside her.

"You're so beautiful," he whispered in her ear.

He withdrew and drove back inside her hitting her most sensitive places, making her cry out in shameless abandon. His mouth covered hers, silencing her. His tongue plunged into her mouth in the same rhythm as his thrusts into her vagina. He continued this strategy and within seconds, the frantic climax built to a feverish pitch.

He thrust harder. Fire zipped through her, destroying all sane thoughts. She smiled at the sound of his sexy grunts as he continued to thrust into her. She arched her hips, allowing him deeper penetration. She teetered on the brink. One last thrust from him was all she needed.

And then she came.

Chapter Seven

Sky exploded. A scream flew from her mouth as she shattered into splinters of pleasure and convulsed beneath him. The frantic euphoria took hold of her and carried her to the pleasure world.

He pumped harder and harder. Faster and faster. Violent waves of pure pleasure jolted her as she writhed. He pumped into her like a fierce storm and she matched his every thrust. Ecstasy snowballed and she hung onto sweet agony for as long as she could. Soon her powerful climax softened into shudders.

Jim continued to piston. She opened her eyes and watched the vulnerability lash his face as he concentrated on his thrusts. An determined smile tipped his lips. His eyes were scrunched tightly. He groaned and shuddered violently as he spilled inside her.

Finally, he went limp, collapsing on top of her. She was satisfied from the lovemaking and buried her face into his warm neck. His pulse hammered against her cheek and a wonderful peace enveloped her.

They were married.

Only minutes ago, she had thought they might have a chance at getting back together and now here she was lying beneath the man she loved, his ring of love on her finger. She smiled into the heat of his neck and drifted off into a hazy world of love and wanting more sex. She must have drifted for a while for when she awoke, Jim wasn't inside her anymore. He lay beside her, cuddling her in his strong arms. He'd removed her cuffs.

"The preacher is gone. He left the marriage license on the table," his warm breath caressed her face.

"Everything's going to be alright now, Sky. He can't hurt us as long as we do as he says. I'll do whatever it takes to protect you and keep you from harm."

"I don't care what he threatens us with. As long as we're together we can withstand anything he throws our way."

He grinned. "Spoken like a true trooper."

Tingling tension zipped inside her as his gaze moved along her naked body. Within a second she was so needy for him, she thought she might explode.

"Now we can start the honeymoon." His velvety voice made cream warmly.

"I love you so much. I'm sorry we fought."

"I'm sure there will be more fights. We're both strong willed. But we'll have some heavy making up sessions, I'm sure."

She reached out, grabbed his shoulders and pulled him down on top of her.

His mouth dominated hers as he clamped tightly over her lips. His tongue wasted no time invading her, plunging past her teeth. He warred with her tongue. His sharp jabs, insistent, sent a yearning clashing between her thighs. His scent overwhelmed her and made her swoon. Made her wonder if maybe she'd bitten off more than she could chew.

The kiss continued. It was hard and long until it took all breath from her lungs. Finally, he ripped his mouth free and he anchored himself on his elbows. His chest heaved against her sensitive nipples, his muscled thighs cradled her and his rod, thick and heavy, was poised at the entrance of her vagina.

He gazed down at her. His eyes were wild with desire. His full mouth red and plump from the kiss.

"I've wanted you so bad for so long and now you're mine," he said.

Heat rose in her cheeks. "I'm sorry I made you wait so long."

In answer, he nipped violently at her bottom lip. She gasped in pain. Tasted her own blood. The bite pulsed erotically.

"You bastard."

His eyes glittered with amusement.

"I could have fucked you on that desk at Sex Squad Headquarters. I could have slid my aching shaft into you. You were so ripe and ready. It would have been so easy."

She shivered at his honesty.

"But I didn't. That's when I knew I wanted you in my life forever. I knew I could wait for you. I want to father your children. I want to fuck you every morning until we are so goddamn old we can't do it anymore. That's my vow to you, Sky. Every morning I'm going to fuck you. Hard. So hard you're going to ache. So hard, you're going to beg me for more. So much you'll remember me wherever you go."

"Only every morning?" she teased.

"Anytime I want. Morning, noon and night."

"What about when I want it?"

He chuckled.

"You'll wear me out if I listen to your wants."

Before she could blink, his lips came crushing down on hers. Intense heat filled her mouth as his tongue plunged deep inside her. Deeper than he'd ever gone before. At the same time, he thrust into her, unleashing a pleasure so wild and so erotic, she had to close her eyes at its intensity.

Instinctively, she lifted her legs and dug the heels of her feet into his muscular ass. The new position allowed him to penetrate deeper. His hardness was a wondrous torture. His length purely monstrous. His thickness, pulsed.

He stopped the impalement and tore his mouth away. He stared down at her. His brown eyes glowed with pride.

"You feel so good wrapped around me. I want to stay inside you forever."

She giggled as happiness flooded her.

"If you do that we'll never have those kids you want."

He lifted a hand and touched a long warm finger to her lips.

"You've got a beautiful mouth, Sky. Lips I need to taste all the time. I can't get enough of you. You tortured me so much, denying me access to you. There were times my water bill left me penniless from all those cold showers."

"With me around, you'll be able to save money. We'll take showers and baths together."

Jim inhaled a deep breath. His rod throbbed inside her. She wanted to gyrate. Wanted him to make love to her.

"I really should punish you for making me wait so long, Sky. I should punish you real hard."

"Punish me?" Excitement slithered up her bare back.

"My penis can bring you pleasure, if I want it to. I can also use it to punish."

Sky gasped as his shaft suddenly pulsated inside her. Her sensitive muscles contracted greedily around his thickness sending an array of pleasant sensations screaming into her womb.

His rod stopped throbbing and her muscles relaxed.

"You son of a bitch!" she gasped. Her pussy ached for more.

"Did you like that?"

"Give me your best shot." She prodded, eager for him to do it again.

The corners of his lips curled upwards. "You don't scare easy do you?"

"I don't have time to be scared, not with your massive punishing tool pulsing inside me. Go ahead, let's see what you're made of."

He chuckled, and then nipped on her bottom lip again. With his tongue he laved the tender bite he'd inflicted earlier. Her flesh sizzled wherever he touched and she shivered. His face curled into the curve her neck and he kissed her there, a feather light kiss she loved. To her surprise, he unexpectedly nipped her hard. Pain sizzled through her neck. She tried to squirm away but his cock held her in place.

"Son of a bitch," she whispered again.

He grinned and winked. "A birthday hickie for the birthday gal. Happy Birthday, Sky."

For crying out loud, she'd forgotten today was her birthday!

He shifted the upper part of his body until his chest rested lightly against her nipples. And then his hands were there, covering both her breasts. His palms kneaded, grabbed and sweetly hurt.

Sky shot him a look of surprise at his roughness. His eyes twinkled with enjoyment and he kissed her cheeks with silky caresses. It was a direct contrast to the way his hands groped her breasts and painfully tweaked her nipples.

"You call this punishment?" she hissed, loving everything he was doing to her.

He rolled his hips and his rod grew harder inside her. Her vaginal muscles quivered. He pulled at her nipples and caught her gasp with his warm mouth. Delightful sensations unfurled along her nerve endings as he kissed her. The vibrations grew, and spread. Flames licked her senses and she writhed beneath him.

"That's it, don't fight it," he whispered.

He drew his hands from her breasts. His chest came down on top of hers. A hand slipped between her legs, and she jolted when he pressed a finger against her clit. His roughness made her pant. Made her moan.

Tension zipped through her.

"Please," she whimpered.

"Please, what?"

"Fuck me."

He didn't say anything and his hand stilled.

Sky moaned.

No! Don't stop!

He didn't move a muscle.

She opened her eyes in time to see the heated expression flare in his eyes. His pulse trembled in his neck as he restrained himself from withdrawing and plunging into her again.

"Please..."

He raised his eyebrows as if surprised by her plea.

"Do you think you've been punished enough?"

"Yes! I can't take it anymore."

It was all he needed to hear. He withdrew plunged right back into her again and teased all her most sensitive areas with his thickness. He rubbed her clit.

He filled her. He fucked her.

She exploded and convulsed. Pure pleasure seared through her crashing over her in a wondrous tidal wave of lust. She squeezed her eyes tighter. The orgasm shuttered through her and she cried out as ecstasy carried her away.

*****

Sky awoke to sunshine streaming in through the farmhouse windows. At first, she didn't know where she was and then reality crashed over her in one wonderful breath sucking wave.

Last night, Jim had married her! He'd made love to her at the same time as Loverboy watched. She stretched her legs and winced at the sweet soreness in her vagina. Pushing aside the sheets, she lifted her left arm and gazed at the gold wedding band.

Warmth enveloped her. She was married to a man she loved with all her heart. A man who'd vowed to fuck her every morning.

And it was morning...So? Where was he?

"Jim!" she called out.

No answer.

The farmhouse was quiet. Deserted? Except for a strange tapping sound coming from somewhere. Sky climbed out of bed and searched for her clothes. They were gone again.

Perhaps Jim was playing games and wanted her to go look for him? She could do that. And when she found him...

She wrapped a sheet around her and tiptoed to the open doorway where she peeked out into the hallway.

Silence. Where was her hubby? Where were all the students? And Loverboy and Carmella?

She walked down the hallway and as she passed the bedrooms she peeked in through the open doorways. All the beds were neatly made. All the rooms were empty. The only sign that anyone had been here were the dozens of unlit candles placed throughout each room.

Downstairs she found a red envelope taped to the inside of the front door.

Dear Sky,

Please find enclosed copies of the wire transfers of the $500,000 into your bank account and another $500,000 dollars into Jim's personal bank account. Now that you are married you can combine your assets. You are both are millionaires. It is up to you if you consider this money as a wedding gift or a bribe.

On the player in the living room you will find three tapes.

One tape is of your trigasm escapade with Jim. One is of your wedding. One shows Jim finger fucking you at Sex Squad Headquarters. These are not the only copies. After viewing them, I trust you will remain silent about the Sex Slave Courses.

If you choose not to remain silent, you will not have the Chief's blessing. It has already been added to your records that you were instructed not to engage in any sexual activity during this assignment. Tsk. Tsk. Tsk. With those three tapes and the bribe, that's four Sex Strikes against you.

Should you break your silence the tapes and the bank receipts will be released to the Sex Squad High Commission. Rest assured the High Commission will ensure your silence. Compliments of me.

Sky's stomach dropped as if she were on an elevator. She'd believed in the Three Sex Strikes and Life policy that was enforced at work. Anyone breaking the Sex rules, one of which was no sex during work hours, had only three chances. When they had three strikes it was off to Sex State Prison for life. Life without sex. Life without Jim.

Jim and she had enough strikes to put them away forever.

She'd voted for the Three Sex Strikes and Life Policy herself. Never in her wildest dreams did she imagine she'd end up having the law used against her in such a way.

Sky cursed softly. Could she trust Loverboy to not release those tapes? It would be in his best interest not to. If he did release them he'd be dragged into the fray. Attention was the last thing Loverboy wanted, especially since he was training Sex Slaves without the government's permission.

Sky nodded at that last thought. Yes, Loverboy would keep quiet. And so would they. No need to get too upset with all this trouble hanging like a guillotine over their heads.

Unbidden came a vision of Jim. Of how he had made her scream last night. She could still remember the rough feel of his callused thumb as he'd frantically kneaded her clit. She remembered the way the round, smooth tip of his massive cock had thrust in and out of her without mercy. He had just about driven her crazy as she convulsed with the several orgasms he'd given her last night. She didn't think she could have had so many.

Obviously, Jim knew how to make love to a woman. And he'd show her so much more of what he was made of on their honeymoon, she was sure of that.

She glanced out the front door's small window. No cars or trucks were in the driveway. Loverboy and everyone else had fled.

No use wearing her toga sheet anymore. She dropped it to the floor and headed into the living room.

The tapes were set on top of the player. All were clearly marked.

Sky studied them and sighed. They'd have to keep these tapes safe and away from prying eyes. She'd have to trust Loverboy to keep his copies safe too.

Dammit! It wasn't the greatest feeling knowing you were set up. But they would survive. They would love each other every day and Jim had promised to fuck her every morning...

That insistent tapping started again. It was coming out of the heating vent and there was a pattern.

Morse Code? Someone was sending her a message?

In the basement. Help.

Where was the basement?

She scanned the living room. Aside from Loverboy's office door, she didn't see any other doors.

Heart pounding, Sky raced into the kitchen and froze. One section of the kitchen wall was pushed aside revealing a secret door.

Turning the doorknob, Sky opened the door to discover a steep staircase, which disappeared into a dimly lit hall. The tapping continued with the same insistent message.

It had to be from Jim. They'd done something to him. They'd hurt him some way.

Terror rushed through her and she couldn't run down the stairs fast enough. When she reached the bottom, she became overwhelmed at all the doors. Gathering her senses she counted three doors on each side of the hallway. The last one to the right was open. Racing down the hallway, Sky peered in.

And gasped at the sight.

Chapter Eight

Sky's new hubby lay on a table. Legs and arms spread eagle and strapped down. He had a ball gag in his mouth, which prevented him from speaking. As she entered, relief soaked his brown eyes.

"They had to tie you down to keep you from running out on me?" she asked.

A chuckle escaped around the ball gag. Circling the table, she examined the sleek muscles of his chest, the tight ripples over his flat stomach and she smiled at Jim's thick vein riddled cock.

"Did they tie you up down here?"

His eyes widened and he moved his head, but she couldn't tell if it was a nod or a shaking of the head as a restraint held his head relatively still.

"Where you being a bad boy?"

He rolled his eyes as if pissed off at the question.

"I get the feeling you came upon them leaving?"

Again, a movement, which should could not understand.

"Well, they're gone now and we're all alone. So, that makes it possible for me to have my way with you."

The instant her fingers curled around his cock, he moaned. His shaft thickened and grew.

"We're free to carry on with our honeymoon." Sky said as she trailed the tips of her fingers up one side of his quickly hardening shaft, over his flushed cockhead and then down the other side.

He wiggled beneath her touch, his cute lips tightening around the ball gag.

"You like this do you?" she teased.

Another innocuous head movement.

"Is that shake of your head a yes? Or a no?" Sky ran her finger back up over his bulging cockhead.

He shuddered.

"I'll have to believe you've nodded a yes, that you do enjoy this."

She bent over until she was face to face with his rigid member and Sky remembered how his cock had throbbed inside her last night. Now it was her turn to give back to her husband a little of what she'd experienced while handcuffed to the bed and then later when he'd taken her so hard.

Payback was going to be a bitch. She smiled and licked her lips in anticipation.

In one open mouthed thrust, she slid her lips over his flushed cockhead. He groaned loudly at the hot assault. He was hard and pulsed against her lips and his hips bucked, shoving him deeper into her mouth.

Sky pursed her lips and began to suck, ever so gently. He moaned a tight, wild sound that sent tingles of excitement shimmering through her. She sucked harder. Jim's hips convulsed and she tasted his pre-come in her mouth.

She liked the taste of him. Liked the taste of man-strength. She sucked harder, and flicked her tongue down along his stiff shaft. His cock tensed. He was ready to come. She stopped and lifted her head. He groaned a growl of protest.

Hmm, how long should she stall him before he became angry enough to give her a good fucking? Oh heck, a little torture was good for a man and his penis.

"How did you make that tapping sound anyway?" she asked.

A furious mumble escaped from around the ball gag.

"Oh yes, I better remove this fun thing. We'll save it for later."

She leaned over and unhooked the ball gag. He pushed it away with his tongue.

"Just fuck me, will you?"

"Not so fast, sweet hubby. Answer my question. How'd you get my attention? Better yet, how did you know I was upstairs?"

"Carmella and Loverboy set me up down here. For you. At my request."

Sky's breath hitched in her throat.

Oh.

"For me?"

"You can do what ever you want to me."

"I kind of get that picture. But why?"

"Because I want you happy. I want you to experience sex in every way. Besides it wasn't fair for you to have been handcuffed to the bed last night."

"I didn't mind at all once the action started."

"You are so beautiful, Sky."

"Cut to the chase, darling. Why this table?"

"It's called the passion rack. I thought maybe we could try this table. Take turns?"

Oh my. The man was going to kill her with all this exciting new stuff. This could develop into one very interesting marriage.

"In answer to your first question. When Loverboy and Carmella strapped me to the table, they told me I'd have to figure out a way on my own to get your attention. By the time I heard you walking around upstairs I'd figured out this ingenious way..." Jim arched his hips upward and then crashed his ass down onto the table with enough force to make the table wiggle, allowing it to give off a loud tap.

She didn't miss the wince on his face when his butt hit the board.

"Lift your ass again," she instructed.

He did as she asked. Sky bent over and noticed the tiny tacks lining the board. Tiny enough so they would cause pain but not big enough to draw blood.

His ass cheeks were red with tiny indentations.

"You're going to need some tender loving care on those cheeks, honey."

The corners of his lips curved upwards into an eager smile.

"But not quite yet. First we're going to give this table a workout."

She examined the tacks and nodded in understanding. "Pain makes the brain secrete endorphins. Endorphins counteract pain and creates pleasure. Very ingenious."

Could she achieve extreme pleasure with Jim, through pain? This question was something to ponder on their honeymoon.

"Can you at least suck me off and give me some relief before you get started?"

"Um, nope."

Jim inhaled a sharp breath as she wrapped both hands around his thick cock, relishing the powerful heat he gave off.

"I still want to taste other parts of you. It might take me some time."

The excruciating expression on Jim's face made Sky laugh. She had the power over him. She could do whatever she wanted to him. Get whatever she wanted. All with his blessing. This power trip was a nice feeling.

"Did Loverboy say when he was coming back?" Sky asked.

Hesitation flashed in his eyes.

"Tell the truth," she coaxed.

"Two weeks. Long enough for a proper honeymoon. His gift to us."

"Good. Very good. This will give us time to acquaint ourselves with each other, shouldn't it?"

Jim nodded. The smile flittered back onto his face again. He was looking forward to getting fucked morning noon and night.

Maybe she should teach him to be careful of what he wished for...

*****

Sky stepped out of Jim's field of vision. Footsteps plodded quietly to the base of the table where he lay. She removed an area of the table between his spread-eagle legs and then she moved in between them. He groaned as she produced a tube of lube and slurped some into her hand. She rubbed her hands gently and then she reached down, her soft, warm hands cupping his ass.

What the hell was she up to?

"Relax my love. There's plenty of cleansing lube to go around."

His heart galloped as her smeared fingers massaged his ass with soothing little circles. Within seconds, his ass cheeks tingled.

Then she casually moved her massages inwards. There was no mistaking where she was headed. Toward the crack in his ass. Soon, her delicate fingers arrived at their destination and Jim waited anxiously to see what would happen next.

With feather light strokes, she traced the entire length of both sides of his crack, ending just beneath his hardening balls.

She retreated with her fingers. He exhaled a shuddering breath. Then she slid back again. Back and forth until the outer edges of his crack were on fire with arousal. He groaned in protest when she stopped.

A moment later, her face pressed intimately into his ass cheeks. The suddenness of it, hell the shock of it, sent his hips soaring upwards and then down onto the board. The tacks bit painfully into his ass.

"Pain heightens the pleasure centers," she said and then laughed.

Something warm and moist pressed against the outside edges of his asshole.

Her tongue! Damned if a woman had ever gone near his ass with her tongue before. It felt strange and oddly exciting.

Jim sucked in another breath as she pulled his ass cheeks wider apart. Wider and yet wider.

Then her tongue began licking the outer edges of his hole. Teasing it with little stabs.

Extraordinary growls drifted to his ears and Jim realized with shock the foreign sound was coming from him! His breathing became labored. Damned if he was enjoying these interesting new sensations shimmering along his skin toward his balls.

He bucked violently when Sky's finger unexpectedly pushed past his tight sphincter muscles. Nerves he never knew existed flickered to life as her lubed finger burrowed inward at an agonizingly slow pace.

He groaned when she stopped. He could feel her deep inside. Could feel his muscles grip tightly around her finger. The alluring intrusion made his ass pulse with wicked pressure.

Her knuckles pressed against the area between his balls, creating a fantastic pressure in his penis and scrotum area. His cock swelled tighter and fuller until it ached.

Slowly, she slipped out her finger. Jim shuddered as she drove in again. This time with two lubed fingers. His ass muscles contracted quickly sucking her fingers deeper inside him. She withdrew again, leaving Jim waiting and wanting more.

Man! Had someone told him he'd be getting finger fucked up his butt, he would have said no way was anyone going near his ass. And here he was responding like a damn pro.

Something cold and hard pressed against his hole making Jim stiffen in alarm.

"Shh. Relax. Trust me. I'm going to insert a butt plug."

A butt plug!

"It's been nicely lubricated and shall go in easily enough now that I've programmed your muscles to receive it."

Gosh, she sounded like a pro already.

"It will increase your pleasure later on," she whispered.

Later on? Jim forced himself to relax his anal muscles as the foreign object slipped into his hole. She pushed it inward.

To his astonishment, his hips began to shake and undulate of their own volition. The result, sharp jabs of pain in his ass cheeks from the tacks on the board. The butt plug was a foreign invasion that kept filling him as he'd never been filled before. A tinge of panic swept over him. How long was this thing? Was it ever going to end?

Suddenly a strange feeling zipped along his anal nerves. It was a quivery sensation and he liked it a lot. She stopped the insertion and his ass felt full and shuddered erotically.

Jim exhaled.

Footsteps echoed through the silence, and Sky strolled up beside the table. She smiled down at him. His heart tightened with love.

"That wasn't too bad, was it?" she said, echoing his earlier thought. "How does it feel?"

"Like something is in my ass," he joked.

"You'll be glad the plug is in considering what I have planned for you."

"And exactly what is that?" He tried to keep the excitement in check.

She said nothing and moved out of his field of vision again. He heard movement somewhere in the far corner of the room, but couldn't see her. Then she began to hum.

"Sky? What are you up to?"

"Just give me a minute. I've got a surprise for you."

The sweet sexy sound of her voice made his heart begin to thump loudly in his ears. He got the feeling he was going to like what she was planning for him.

A minute later, something slid across the floor toward his right side. Her warm arm curled across his waist as Sky hoisted herself up onto the table. Her breasts swayed as she stood up and placed her legs wide apart touching the outside of his shoulders. It gave him a damned fascinating view of her pussy.

"You like what you see?" She purred as she gazed down at him.

"Holy shit," he breathed.

His balls tightened even more, if that were possible. His shaft became so rigid he was sure he'd come at any second.

He'd read somewhere that a guy's brains were wired differently than a woman's. Women became sexually stimulated when they were cuddled and told warm, fuzzy things. Men, on the other hand became sexually excited by something visual.

Gazing straight up into Sky's pussy was definitely visual. And sexually stimulating.

"Pleasure me, slave," she demanded and she began to squat.

His mouth watered as her pussy lowered into just the right position over his face. Using his tongue, he pried apart her swollen lips, and zeroed upward onto her clit. As he circled her clit with slow torturous jabs, she gasped and whimpered her appreciation.

Since she'd had a little bit of fun torturing him earlier, perhaps he should return the favor...

"You taste so damn good, Sky."

"Tongue fuck me, Jim." Her voice sounded tortured. Raw. Sensual. Beautiful.

He closed his eyes and probed around her sweet heat, taking his time as he circled her clit in torturous circles. Her thighs quivered and she pressed her pussy against his face. He gyrated his hips as he imagined his thick shaft replacing his tongue as he speared into her warm, wet vagina.

The butt plug created some fantastic sensations, sparking a cascade of spasms in his ass. Whiffs of her sex made him heady and his body hardened with need. The woman was killing him by denying his cock access to her pussy. He would pay her back big time.

A high-pitched wail broke from her and ripped through the air. Arching her hips into his face, she climaxed, marking him with her sexy scent. When she came down from her high, she lifted herself from his face. On trembling legs, she stood once again giving him a perfect view of her pussy.

Jim shivered with frustration. His rod was hard enough it could drill holes. He was ready to fuck her. His breath came in shallow spurts. His heart pounded and he anxiously waited to see what Sky was going to do next.

"You are an exquisite lover, my slave," she praised. "And now you shall be rewarded."

When her velvety hand wrapped firmly around the base of his shaft, his cock shuddered violently. Her moist warm mouth welcomed him and Jim groaned as her lips firmly encased his hard flesh.

He groaned as her sweet tongue slid erotically against the underneath part of his rod. His scrotum grew tight and his shaft hardened with excruciating need.

She sucked. His whole body blew apart.

He thrust his hips upward, making his cock sink deeper into her moist mouth. Her tongue curled erotically against his shaft. He dropped back onto the passion rack and the tacks rammed into his sensitive skin causing mild pain to sear his ass cheeks. The butt plug lodged deeper into his ass causing sparkling sensations that ripped through him.

The woman sure knew how to torture him.

His body was tight with need. The pressure in his cock and balls were fantastic.

She continued to suck. Her warm lips sealed his shaft as if it were her prisoner. One hand tightened around his base and her other hand flew to his scrotum area, were she kneaded his balls until he could stand it no longer.

"Sky!" he managed to gasp in warning.

Slurping sounds wrent the air as she continued sucking.

He couldn't wait. Couldn't hold on any longer. The need for release was too overpowering.

Jim cut loose, surprised that she swallowed as quickly as he came.

*****

Sky smiled at Jim's relaxed features as he lay on the passion table. He was panting and his chest was heaving after she'd made love to his cock with her mouth.

"You're becoming a pro at this," he breathed.

"I'll take that as a compliment."

"You've wiped me out."

Disappointment shot through her.

"Are you saying you're ready to call it quits? Have some breakfast and pick this up later?"

"No way. We trade places." Jim cooed. "And I'm going to give you the fucking of your life."

"You are, are you? I like the sound of that." She laughed and eagerly untied his restraints.

"I want to hear your screams when I make you come, Sky. It's a good thing we're out here in the middle of nowhere, because I'm going to make you come so many times, the windows are going to shatter."

"Keep talking that way, big guy and I'll be coming before you even start."

"Come here," he whispered.

He curled his arms around her waist, guiding her down on top of his naked body. Sweet hunger gripped her insides as his hard contours snuggled her soft curves. She loved the feel of his skin touching hers. Loved the ache throbbing deep inside her vagina as his rapidly reviving cock pushed intimately between her legs.

"Have I told you how much I love you this morning?" he whispered. His eyes darkened as he awaited her answer.

"I don't think so."

"I love you, Sky. Every minute that goes by I feel it growing."

Sky laughed.

His eyes darkened in surprise. "I tell my woman I love her and she laughs. What's so funny?"

"You're growing all right," she muttered.

Slowly she slid her hands down the sides of his hard lean waist, loving the muscular planes beneath her fingertips as she slowly headed for his blossoming shaft.

"I hate to break this mood," she whispered and gently bit his lower lip. "But what are we going to do about Loverboy? And all this stuff he has hanging over our heads?"

"We wait."

"That's what I figured we should do."

His hands slid from her waist to cup the back of her neck.

"That doesn't mean we'll do anything he wants us to do. You have to remember he won't release those tapes. Not unless he wants to incriminate himself. So we're safe as long as we keep our mouths shut."

"I can do that." Sky nibbled his upper lip. His hard body shivered with excitement below her.

"Rest assured I won't stop trying to find a way to get his copies of us together," he said.

"It's just going to take some time. Maybe years. In the meantime, don't touch any of the money he placed in our accounts. It's evidence."

"You're reading my mind." She curled her lips along the warmth of his neck. The pounding of his pulse quickened as her hands slid around his thickening erection. She loved the wonderful power running through his cock.

"Uh, uh. Not yet. Are you reading my mind?" he groaned against her ear.

"My turn on the rack?"

"Damn straight."

He clamped his mouth over hers. The heat of his lips sliding over hers was heavy with promises of things to come. This was going to be one hell of a honeymoon.

The End

Newsletter

Hi! If you would like to get an email when my books are released, you can sign up here:

Newsletter: http://ymlp.com/xguembmugmgb

Your emails will never be shared and you can unsubscribe whenever you like.

Discover Some Other Titles by Jan Springer

Ménage - Book 1

Sandwiched between constant deadlines and suffering a bad case of writer's block, erotic romance author, Claire Miller, decides it's time to unwind with a sensual ménage at The Key Club. When she's paired with a couple of well-hung hunks, she knows they'll make her naughtiest dreams come true.

Instant attraction make Josh and Levis take notice of the timid woman at the Club. She's a hot dream the two men can't wait to experience, and their desire for Claire becomes a pleasure they don't want to escape.

Marley's Ménage – Book 2

Single, soon-to-be mom, Marley Madison, is having some very naughty cravings. She wants a ménage and she needs it bad. When she gets word her local swinger's club is having a ménage night specifically for pregnant women, count her in!

Marley's ex-flames Rick Antonia and Kacey Poole have just gotten back to town after serving in the Special Ops for many years. When the two men spot Marley at the Key Club, they can't believe how much she's changed. Her sweetly rounded belly arouses them and her curvy breasts intrigue them. They want her back in their bed and they're going to make sure her dream of a scorching ménage comes true!

Suddenly Marley is pleasure bound and shocked that her two ex-lovers are as passionate as ever. She's never been so aroused by their caring touches and tender kisses...but Marley was in love with them years ago and she's vowed not to let that complication happen again...

A Merry Christmas Ménage - Book 3

Dr. Kelsie Madison can't remember the last time she's had no-strings sex and that's her clue she's been working way too hard. It's time to unwind at the Key Club by indulging in a yummy Christmas present for herself. Something she's never experienced before - a red-hot ménage.

ER Dr. Ryder Greene and his roommate, physiotherapist, Dixon Flynn love sharing their women. They've had their eye on cute Dr. Kelsie Madison for quite some time, but she's a workaholic and she never has time to play.

When they learn she'll be at the *Santa Claus Ménage Night* festivities, they'll make sure they're the ones kissing Kelsie under the mistletoe. And if they get their wish, Kelsie will be taking them home for Christmas.

Sophie's Ménage – Book 4

It's *Spank-Me Ménage Night* at the Key Club and Sophie is finally taking the plunge back into the scene. She didn't count on her two hunky ex-flames to be there or for their renewed interest in her. They're the only men who could ever make her climax, but she's determined not to submit to her naughty desires where they're concerned, especially after the way they'd left her. Surely a bit of harmless teasing wouldn't hurt in order to show them what they could have had...

Oil rig workers Steve and Eric are back in Alberta and they can't wait to bend the sweet, timid hairstylist over their knees to give her the sensual spankings she craves. But the surprise is on them when they catch her wearing a sexy spank dress while auctioning herself to the highest bidder. Who knew the shy little firecracker could be such a sultry tease? Or that she wasn't going to be easily led back to their bed...

Jewel's Ménage - Book 5

She thought she would never trust a man again...

Until one rainy night, two hunky truckers come to Jewel's rescue, igniting red-hot fantasies of a ménage à trois. When she can no longer deny the sensual needs burning deep inside, she knows it's time to bury her past and pamper herself within the searing heat and incredible pleasure she'd once experienced at The Key Club.

Bring Your Own Toys Ménage Night is coming to The Key Club and truckers Carson and Adam plan to seduce Jewel out of her mistrust of men and thrust her into an erotic-filled evening of exquisite submission. They'll do it with the alluring usage of pleasure toys, silky bondage ties and plenty of red-hot love.

Jaxie's Ménage - Book 6

A close encounter with death pushes Jaxie into making one of her most intimate fantasies come true.

Never one for mixing business with pleasure, Jaxie Smarts knows it's time to break that rule. With the help of one of her best friends, they'll make sure Jaxie gets the two sexiest hunks at the Masquerade Ménage Ball. But Jaxie's well-laid plans quickly unravel...

When Ewan's best friend, Royce, drags Ewan to the Key Club's Masquerade Ménage Ball, he's only going because he knows Jaxie won't be there. Saving her life is one thing, but having his heart broken over and over by her is quite another. He's sworn himself off Jaxie. Forever.

At the Ball, a seductive princess bride wearing a sexy mask captures his attention, unleashing a deep craving that lures Ewan and Royce to use the Key Club's trick hat to get her into their ménage bed. The last thing Ewan expects is to fall in love all over again.

Some Other Titles by Jan Springer (Series and Stand Alones)

Series

The Desperadoes series (Post-Catastrophic Erotic Romance Menage)

A fiery eruption of solar flares disintegrates most of Earth's human population, frying electrical grids around the world and thrusting everyone into a cold, harsh land where only the strong survive...

The Pleasure Girl – Book One

Forced to become a pleasure girl in order to survive, Teyla Sutton reluctantly agrees to service dangerous desperado Logan Leigh and his two friends. White-hot pleasure becomes addictive beneath Logan's tender touches and his hard, muscular body. What Teyla never expected was to fall in love.

Logan knows he shouldn't allow the Pleasure Girl into his heart, but he also knows it's too late because she's already there. Soon three desperadoes are whisking Teyla away on an exquisite journey into her hottest dreams and forbidden desires. When she learns they are members of the notorious Durango Gang, can she allow them into her life, or will she send them away forever?

In Her Bed – Book Two

Before the Catastrophe, Dr. Elizabeth Brandywine would never have dreamed of actually surrendering to her wicked needs of being bound, dominated, and shared, but now there's no one left alive to judge her, except herself.

Ethan Durango knows sweet, uptight, sexy Dr. Liz is ready to submit to her secret sexual needs. Hes always wanted to share her. To have her tied up while he and his friends take her. Ethan, Landon, and Tyrell will enjoy seducing Liz past her boundaries until she submits to her naughtiest desires.

Be My Dream Tonight – Book Three

Passionate ménages with the fierce men of the Durango gang have always made Eve Wright's body hum with sizzling arousal. Secretly, she loved all three men, that is, until she suffered a head injury and forgot them. Now her memory is returning with a carnal vengeance and she knows of only one way to relieve her sexual frustrations...by returning to the men she once loved.

When Eve shows up at their hideout, Kayne, Riley, and Maddox are pleased she wants them to help her remember what they once shared.

Their hot looks, tender touches, and scorching pleasure-pain leaves Eve tangled in an erotic storm that threatens to break her heart and give up a gut-wrenching secret.

Stand-alone titles

Toygasm (Contemporary Erotic Romance Menage)

It's a case of mistaken identity when identical twin brothers Josh and Jode Midnight, owners of Sexy Toys, show up for an erotic photo shoot of their toys with famous nude model Cammie Creek.

Cammie believes the two well-hung hunks are the men she's supposed to pose with. Usually she doesn't mix business with pleasure but when they're seducing her right in front of the cameras and delivering the best orgasms she's ever experienced, she can't resist turning them into her personal sex toys.

Josh and Jode can't get enough of Cammie—hot lust, sizzling toys and the best sex they've ever had. But how will she react when she discovers they're actually her bosses and that they fell in love with her before they'd even met her?

Edible Delights (Contemporary Erotic Romance Menage)

Years ago Allie Masters lost herself in the scorching passion of a ménage a trois relationship with her two striking bosses. In order to regain her independence, she walked away.Max and Nick were very fulfilled with their gorgeous redheaded assistant. The lovemaking was breathtaking and both friends willingly shared the woman they wanted to spend the rest of their lives with. And then she left.Now Max and Nick have decided it's time to seduce Allie back into their lives.

Sinderella (Contemporary Erotic Romance with voyeurism)

By day she's a dedicated gynecologist. By night Dr. Ella Cinder escapes reality by secretly performing in her own erotic, adult version of Cinderella, aptly re-titled Sinderella. When sexy colleague Dr. Roarke Stephenson shows up in the Sinderella audience on the same night her

Prince Charming stands her up, Ella seizes the opportunity to make Roarke into her Prince Charming for one carnal night of hot, blazing sex...in front of an audience.

But at the strike of midnight, Ella knows she must face the harsh reality that Roarke must never learn her secret life and they can never be together again. Until then, she plans on making sure he'll never forget their night of carnal play.

Dr. Roarke Stephenson is immediately captured by the lusciously curvy actress who hides behind a mask and is known only as Sinderella. For some insane reason she reminds him of his klutzy co-worker Ella. But that's not possible. Ella would never have the nerve to do the wickedly delicious things Sinderella does to him...or would she?

Her Captive (Contemporary Erotic Romance)

Her perfect lover...

Modern day pirate Morgan Black's life has always been immersed in the violent and traditional ways of piracy. When her family's arch enemy puts a hit on her family, Morgan knows there's one sure way to lift the hit; she must kidnap their enemy's sexy grandson and literally force a union between the two warring families. Night after night, wrapped in Roman's strong arms, she can't deny the searing attraction blazing between them. Nor can she deny he now holds her heart as well as her life in his hands.

His dream angel...

When Roman Prince's captor offers him her luscious body, fierce desire ignites, melting his usually tight self-control. Lust quickly turns to love as he enjoys their naughty sexual trysts more than he knows he should. But how will he react when he discovers he's been kidnapped, not for a ransom, but for his sperm?

Let's Get Physical (Contemporary Erotic Romance with ménage scenes)

When the local swingers' club throws a Medical Fetish Night Before Xmas party for charity, Roxie learns that scrumptious blue-collar worker Evan Johnston will be playing doctor...

And he's offering one lucky lady an erotic sexual exam—along with a sizzling ménage e trois.

Roxie is desperate to be his patient. There's no better way to intimately know the guy who's stolen her heart than by hopping on the gyno table for the hottest physical of her life.

The Biker and The Bride (Contemporary Erotic Romance)

Wrapped in red-hot lust for revenge, Avery plots to murder the man responsible for the death of her son.

Her plans are dashed when her ex-husband crashes her wedding and whisks her away on his motorcycle to the rustic Canadian wilderness cabin they'd once honeymooned.

Police detective, Mason is fighting for Avery's love with everything he has.

Armed with whipped cream, handcuffs and his undying devotion, Mason vows he will make Avery love again.

But it's only a matter of time before the man she'd planned to kill hunts them down...

Club Rendezvous (Contemporary Erotic Romance with ménage scenes)

(in the Ellora's Cavemen Legendary Tails II anthology)

Finally free of an abusive relationship, "Shy Girl" Emma McCall sheds her inhibitions and explores her sexual side at Club Rendezvous, a swinger's club specializing in the Alternate Lifestyle. Here she meets up with the dashing Logan Masters, a sexy hunk she's secretly fantasized about since college. With the help of his gorgeous twin brother, Luke, Emma will experience her ultimate fantasy...a scorching ménage a trois.

Nice Girl Naughty (Contemporary Erotic Romantic Suspense)

Blind since nineteen, Summer has blossomed into a famous wood carver, her talented hands giving life to erotic art. When her own life is nearly taken by a serial killer, she finds herself suddenly whisked to a secluded wilderness cabin by sexy bodyguard Nick.

Summer can't get enough of touching Nick's thick, powerful muscles and all those other hard, yummy male body parts. It doesn't take long before the cabin's every surface—horizontal or vertical—is marked by their scorching lovemaking.

For years Nick has stayed away from nice girl Summer. Now he's back, and sweeping his gorgeous redhead into the naughty, erotic sex-fest they've been craving for years. With passion blinding him, Nick doesn't realize their hideout isn't safe—until it's too late.

Claiming Hannah (Futuristic Erotic Romance)

(formerly A Hitman for Hannah)

Hannah is a Breeding Slave. Created solely for the purpose of producing healthy offspring for an ailing human race, Hannah Roberts longs for freedom and fantasizes about the dangerous man she can never have. With her breeding status about to commence, her hunger for freedom explodes. Escaping into the night, she knows capture will bring her certain death.

Jacob is her Hitman. Trained to be a cold-blooded killing machine, the only light in Jacob Romero's life is Hannah, a beautiful Slave whose sweet innocence brands his heart and awakens dark desires he never knew he had. Assigned to hunt her down and kill her, he's seriously injured when he saves her life.

Forbidden love always finds a way. Now fugitives, they hide in a deserted mansion where Hannah nurses the wounded Hitman she's always wanted. Soon their passions ignite, throwing them into a sexual ecstasy neither can run from. Their forbidden love will face one final challenge. Escaping to a harsh new life in the Free States.

Sexual Release (Fantasy Erotic Romance Ménage)

Princess Mica of Azar is approaching her thirtieth birthday. It's a time when an Azarian woman begins her cravings for Sexual Release with one or more males. Because she lives all alone on her planet, Mica has created a very special birthday present for herself—two full-grown stud clones made in the images of her childhood friends, Dakota and Nathan, humans who were captured and taken away as slaves years ago.

They were her best friends yet she was forbidden to love them, compliments of Azar's Purity Law. With her newly created sexy clone studs, she is planning to release the fires that rage within.

Dakota and Nathan have finally managed to escape their captors and return to make Princess Mica their mate. But how will she react when she discovers they've taken the place of her precious clones and that they won't be taking orders from her?

Reader Advisory: Story contains a scene that includes male/male erotic interaction.

Pleasure for Him (Contemporary Erotic Romance with ménage scenes)

Billionaire Spa-franchise owner Ryland Walton wants to give his girlfriend, Lily, a gift of pleasure that only more than one man can give to a woman.

When interior decorator Lily Tiffany receives a diamond-encrusted key with an invitation to a private island estate, she's both nervous and excited that her sexy boyfriend is once again surrendering her to his dark desire of sharing her with another man.

Attracted to Her (f/f contemporary erotic romance)

Millionaire sex-toy creator Aniston is on a mission. She's going to crack the icy exterior of her best customer's assistant Madilyn and melt her heart if it's the last thing she does. Her tempting strategy includes her glass chateau in the Colorado Rockies, a bit of bondage, toys she's whipped up especially for Madilyn and lots of erotic pleasure.

Relationship-shy Madilyn has kept her intense attraction to Aniston hidden behind her cool exterior. After a disastrous breakup with her first—and only—girlfriend, she's not interested in risking her heart again, no matter how sexy the other woman is.

Attracted to Him (m/m erotic romance)

Newly single billionaire Daniel Knight has it all—luxurious estates, a successful company—and a whole lot of stress. After his personal physician orders Daniel to take a vacation, he takes off for his compound in the Virgin Islands.

Dr. Sander Jonas has lusted after his patient for years but due to a pesky sense of professional ethics—not to mention Daniel's former boyfriend—he's never made a move on him. But when Daniel is injured while swimming, Sander frantically rushes to his boss's aid and finally gives in to the overwhelming attraction he's kept hidden for too many years.

Will scorching water sex with custom-made adult toys, hot, loving nights surrounded by lush palm trees and white sandy beaches prove to be exactly what the doctor ordered to heal Daniel's wounded heart?

~*~

For More eBooks and Print Books visit http://www.janspringer.com

~

About The Author

Jan Springer writes full-time at her home nestled in Ontario, Canada's picturesque cottage country. She enjoys hiking, kayaking, gardening, reading and writing.

She is a member of the Writers Union of Canada, Romance Writers of America and Passionate Ink. She loves hearing from her readers.

A Word From The Author

Hi! Thank you for purchasing this book. Word of mouth is important for any author to succeed. If you enjoyed this story feel free to leave a short review at the place where you bought it. I would really appreciate it. I look forward to bringing you more stories in the near future.

If you would like to contact me directly or personally send me feedback, you can reach me at janspringerauthor@gmail.com

Here are other ways we can connect:

Jan Springer Website at http://www.janspringer.com

Facebook - https://www.facebook.com/janspringereroticromance

Twitter - https://twitter.com/janspringer @janspringer

Pinterest - http://www.pinterest.com/janspringer1/

Jan's Blog - http://janspringerauthor.wordpress.com/blog-2/

LinkedIn: http://ca.linkedin.com/in/janspringerauthor/

Jan 's Newsletter: http://ymlp.com/xguembmugmgb

Google Plus: https://plus.google.com/u/0/101527334949931513035/posts

Goodreads: https://www.goodreads.com/janspringer

Hugs & Happy Reading,
jan springer

Don't miss out!

Visit the website below and you can sign up to receive emails whenever Jan Springer publishes a new book. There's no charge and no obligation.

https://books2read.com/r/B-A-WGQ-XISG

BOOKS 2 READ

Connecting independent readers to independent writers.

Also by Jan Springer

Cowboys Online
Cowboys for Christmas
Cowboys In Her Pocket
Loving Her Cowboys
Cowboys in Her Heart
Always Her Cowboys

Intimate Secrets
Intimate Lover
Intimate Kisses

Kidnap Fantasies
Jade's Fantasy
Zero To Sexy
Christmas Lovers

Pleasure Bound
A Hero's Welcome

A Hero Escapes
A Hero Betrayed
A Hero's Kiss
A Hero Wanted
Captive Heroes

Pleasure Bound Boxed Set
Pleasure Bound : COMPLETE SERIES SciFi Erotic Romance Boxed Set

Tentacles Shifter Erotic Romance
Taken by Him

The Key Club
A Merry Menage Christmas
Sophie's Menage
Jewel's Menage
Jaxie's Menage
A Homecoming Menage Christmas

The Outlaw Lovers
Jude
The Claiming
Colter's Revenge
Tyler's Woman
Resistance

The Outlaw Lovers
Alpha Outlaws Boxed Set

Vampira
Sweet Heat
Wet Heat
Crimson Heat

Standalone
A Touch of Menage Boxed Set
Shades of Menage Boxed Set
Naughty Girl Desires Boxed Set
Nice Girl Naughty
Sinderella Sexy
The Biker and The Bride
The Fire Within
Bared to Him
Pleasure Bound : A Futuristic Adult Romance Boxed Set
Merry Menage Kisses Boxed Set
Stripped Naked
Risqué Girl Delights Boxed Set
A Holiday Menage
Ménage À Trois
A Hitman for Hannah
Billionaire Boyfriend

Watch for more at www.janspringer.com.

About the Author

New York Times & USA Today Best Selling Author Jan Springer writes erotic romances for Spunky Girl Publishing, Ellora's Cave, Totally Bound, Siren Bookstrand and Pocket Books.She lives in Ontario, Canada on four acres of secluded wilderness.Jan enjoys gardening, hiking, kayaking, reading and writing. She is a member of the Writers Union of Canada and Romance Writers of America.

Read more at www.janspringer.com.

www.Ingramcontent.com/pod-product-compliance
Lightning Source LLC
Chambersburg PA
CBHW030544130626
46552CB00006B/2416